"He's a bonny lad,"

Sydney said as he stepped forward and reached a forefinger towards one of Harry's wildly flailing fists.

"If he were as homely as a mud pie, my lord," Miss Fairfax declared with feeling, "he should engage our tenderest sympathy equally as much!"

Despite himself, Sydney was stirred by Miss Fairfax's words. "A point well taken, Miss Fairfax," he conceded. "I believe there is no harm in trying to locate its...rather, *Harry's* mother."

He was rewarded by Miss Fairfax's simple smile which transformed her expression into something celestial. He could almost detect a halo!

Sydney sighed. He had anticipated a tedious three weeks. But he began to suspect that it might be preferable to be bored than to be suddenly confronted with an abandoned babe and a determined angel of mercy called Angela, both of whom were too charming by half!

A HEAVENLY HOUSEGUEST

EMILY DALTON

Harlequin Books

TORONTO • NEW YORK • LONDON
AMSTERDAM • PARIS • SYDNEY • HAMBURG
STOCKHOLM • ATHENS • TOKYO • MILAN
MADRID • WARSAW • BUDAPEST • AUCKLAND

With boundless thanks to my critique group, Lisa,
Lyn and Sharilyn, three classy ladies and dear,
crazy friends with whom I can be entirely myself.
And to Betina, whose delightful, broad mind has
helped stretch mine to new and exciting
possibilities.

Published February 1992

ISBN 0-373-31168-0

A HEAVENLY HOUSEGUEST

PROLOGUE

September 1817

PERCIVAL, LORD AMESBURY, heaved himself along the dark gallery, the single candle he held in his soft, pudgy hand flickering and swirling with each laboured movement. His nightshirt was stretched taut across his ample, middle-aged belly and his nightcap was pulled low on his forehead, as if he thought such a ploy might shield him from recognition, should he be caught skulking about the corridors.

Presently he approached a door, tested the latch and found it unlocked. Smiling, and opening the door only a little, he slid his portly self through and entered the room. As he lifted his rheumy eyes to the large bed set upon a dais in the middle of the chamber, his smile broadened. By the light of a small candelabrum, he perceived Madeline St. James, the dowager Marchioness of Brynne, awaiting him. Her diminutive form was almost lost in the mountain of pillows and cushions plumped up all about her, but her shining blond hair, sparkling blue eyes and blushing cheeks stood out amidst the satin bedclothes.

Lord Amesbury sighed happily. He knew the lady's blond hair came from a bottle of dye, her glowing cheeks from a pot of rouge and her sparkling eyes from too much wine at dinner, but he loved her all the same. Indeed, by morning light she would look rather a fright, he supposed. But he'd be gone to his own bedchamber by then, and he would not see her again until she'd repaired her face from the passions and slumber of the night before.

"Percy, my sleek stallion!" cooed the dowager, stretching forth both dainty arms in welcome.

Lord Amesbury turned and locked the door behind him, then galumphed eagerly towards the bed. He flipped up the blankets and bounced down next to the dowager, immediately clasping her to him and pressing urgent kisses in the general vicinity of her mouth.

"Whoa, my steed!" exclaimed the dowager, laughing and pushing her tiny, bejewelled hands against his heaving chest. "We must talk tonight, Percy. Indeed, we must!"

"Oh, Maddy, must we? I've hardly been able to keep my hands off you all day, dumpling!" Lord Amesbury's heavy jowls drooped pathetically.

The dowager smiled coquettishly, not the least offended that his lordship's pet names for her conjured up visions of food. Indeed, her pet names for him were rather incongruous, as well.

"You know we must talk, Percy. Tomorrow we leave Lynley Hall and our dear friend the countess's hospitality behind us. My son departs from London in a few days and I must return to Castlerigg Abbey to bear him company."

"Good God, Maddy, your son is two-and-thirty! I should think he could take care of himself by now!"

"You know very well why I must return to the Abbey. Without the diversions of London, Sydney grows quite melancholy. In Town, you know, he has a great many friends and activities to support his spirits!"

"Dashed too many, if you ask me," grumbled Lord Amesbury. "One of your son's parties was talked about the whole Season last year. Something about a trapeze suspended from the balusters and a certain Cyprian who goes by the name of Nimble-toes. . . ."

The dowager blushed delicately. "Never mind that, if you please! I shall be the first to admit that Sydney has grown rather wild since he lost his wife, and he—"

"That was two years ago, my sweet! Can the fellow be grieving still?"

"Not so that it can be observed by the generality. And I'm quite sure he has flung himself into such a dissipated mode of life because he does not wish to think. It is too painful for him! He loved her very much, you know. And when he's at the Abbey, where he was so very happy with Caroline, he tends to brood."

"What about the boy? Isn't the boy company to him?"

"You must remember, Percy, Wellesley is old enough now to go to Eton and is only home on holidays."

"What about house parties and such the like?"

"He never invites anyone to the Abbey unless I ask him to. I dareswear, Percy, if I were not there to plague him he would become an absolute hermit while he resides in the country! And then he becomes so blue-devilled that the servants fret themselves sick over him!"

"What are you saying, my pigeon?" wailed Lord Amesbury. "That you cannot marry me? Certainly I am at least as important to you as the comfort of the Abbey servants!"

"Of course, you are! But I cannot abandon my son, either, Percy. Nor will I ever give up hope that Sydney can be made to see the folly of his ways. Someday he will look back and wish he had started another family. But he does not think he shall ever fall in love again. Foolish boy!"

"One's never too old to fall in love, eh, my plump partridge?"

"Indeed not, Percy! But we must convince him of it. I've been thinking..."

Lord Amesbury eyed his beloved warily. "What have you been thinking, pumpkin?"

"I've been thinking about your daughter, Angela!"

"Good God, how could one think of my Angela and your harem-scarem son in the same moment!" expostulated Lord Amesbury, considerably ruffled. "What has one to do with the other?"

"She's a lovely girl, you said, and saintly and sweet into the bargain. The veriest angel with a soul to match, you said. Such a paragon of beauty and virtue ought to be quite irresistible! Mayhap if you came to the Abbey for a visit, bringing Angela with you, Sydney might fall in love with her and cease his wicked ways!"

"More likely he would seduce my innocent angel and leave her with child! Then I would have to kill him, Maddy, and flee the country. We'd *never* be able to marry, then!"

"Percy, you run away with yourself!" returned the dowager, highly offended. "My son is not a monster! He does not deflower innocents! And if you do not choose to believe me on this point, I shall be much put out with you!"

Lord Amesbury felt himself with his back to the wall. Indeed, he had no desire to return to his bed-chamber without pleasuring his comely Maddy one more night before their separation. But the idea of exposing his sweet Angela to a rake like Lord Brynne positively twisted his spleen!

"I promised her a Season, Maddy! She's scarce clapped eyes on any truly eligible men in her short life. Like any young girl, she wants to go to London."

Lady Brynne clicked her tongue. "Since Angela is your only daughter, Percy, you don't know how dreadful a Season can be! Establishing your sons was nothing compared to the exertions you shall endure finding a suitable husband for Angela. You have no notion how fatiguing it will be simply guarding her from the scoundrels and fortune-hunters London has such an abundance of! Not to mention all the truly good men she will draw like bees to honey! You will have to give them each a hearing. A dreadful business, Percy, simply dreadful!''

Being of a basically indolent nature, Lord Amesbury groaned. "But what if your son did marry my Angela and led her a devilish life, Maddy? No comfort or happiness of mine could atone for that, I assure you!''

"Sydney was a devoted husband once. I'm quite sure he can be so again, if the girl is worthy of him.'' At the indignant swelling of Lord Amesbury's chest, the dowager quickly added, "And we both know how very worthy your dear Angela is, don't we? I promise you, once they are married he will be as docile as a kitten!''

"And what if they should *not* marry?'' countered Lord Amesbury, still not convinced.

"Then we shall have to try again with some other girl until Sydney is married to *someone!* Until he is safely wed, I dare not leave him to his own devices. In the meantime, while you are visiting Castlerigg Abbey, I'll be just down the hall from you, my tiger!'' The dowager accentuated her point by pulling off Lord Amesbury's nightcap and sensuously threading her fingers through his thinning grey hair.

Quivering with desire, Lord Amesbury weakened. 'Twas true: if he took Angela to Castlerigg, at least he could be near Maddy for a time and spend more such blissful nights in her arms. And his Angela was such an innocent little lamb that it seemed highly unlikely she would succumb to, or even understand, Lord

Brynne's seductive charms, should he decide to employ them. Indeed, perhaps the jaded marquess would be put off by her obvious purity.

On the other hand, he might be entranced by Angela and fall in love with her, just as the marchioness hoped. And if things went in such a desirable direction, Lord Amesbury would be spared the tedious chore of launching his dearest child into Society.

"What do you say, my love?" purred Maddy, snuggling against him. "Will you bring Angela to the Abbey?"

Spinning into oblivion when Maddy caught his fat earlobe between her neat little teeth, he said, "As you please, my pudding!" Then, before giving himself up completely to passion, he reasoned that if Sydney St. James, the Marquess of Brynne, so much as touched his sweet Angela, he would quite simply run him through with a sword. Satisfied at last, he pulled the dowager to him in a crushing embrace.

"Percy," she sighed contentedly, "you're such a beast!"

CHAPTER ONE

SYDNEY ST. JAMES, Marquess of Brynne, lifted the back of his hand briefly to his mouth to stifle the beginnings of a yawn. Then he slid it beneath the table to stroke the massive head of his dog, resting, as it was, on his thigh. Outside, rain drummed relentlessly against the windows of his elegant dining chamber. He sighed. The prospect of entertaining for three weeks the assortment of people seated at his table was daunting.

His mother had invited Lord Amesbury and his daughter up from Sussex for a rustic sojourn at Castlerigg Abbey, ostensibly in repayment for a visit she'd made the baron when his wife was still alive, some three years past. But Sydney knew full well that *that* excuse quite simply was a bag of moonshine! His mother was an inveterate matchmaker. Despite the fact that Sydney had been very happily married before and had an heir and therefore no inclination or need to marry again, the dowager marchioness would not give up. She was convinced that her only son was wasting away his life in dissipation.

Sydney sifted long fingers through his thick crop of dark curly hair. Indeed, perhaps he *was* wallowing chin deep in the less elevating pleasures of life these days, but he was hurting no one in the process, after all. He behaved very well at the Abbey, where he was eager to provide a fitting atmosphere for his growing son, Wellesley, and also because he wished to engender trust and good will amongst his quiet-living neighbours and tenants. In London, however, he felt it very much his own business how he conducted himself and with whom he chose to associate.

Obviously his mother disagreed with this sort of hedonistic logic, or else why would she bring home a young woman who fairly oozed purity? Angela Fairfax was aptly named, for, indeed, if he ever imagined an angel, it would be like her. All in white muslin and white satin ribbons, with a little edge of demure lace at her high-necked bodice, with dainty cream-coloured, rose-embroidered slippers peeking out from under her flounced hem, Angela Fairfax looked fit to serve at St. Peter's right hand, welcoming the elect to heaven.

And if her heavenly attire did not convince one that she might sprout wings at any moment, her face and figure could not fail to do so. Of slightly less than medium height, Miss Fairfax was plump and rounded in all the right places and a mere hands' breadth at the waist. It made one fervently wish to catch a glimpse of her ankles, for they were bound to be as neat as wax, and Sydney had a passion for trim ankles.

As for her face…well, it was seraphic, ethereal. Her skin was white and translucent, like a wisp of cloud. Her eyes were the clear grey of the breast of a dove.

Her countenance was soft and regular, like a painted
Madonna's, but with two charming exceptions. A
slightly *retroussé* nose and a stubborn little chin gave
her otherwise classical features an intriguing particu-
larity. And to top this gamine beauty was a tumble of
golden curls Venus might have envied.

He had grown quite poetic, thought Sydney wryly,
eyeing the paragon beside him. Regrettably, he found
these charming attractions altogether insipid. For
without a mind and a spirit to match, what good was
beauty, after all? And Sydney had never met a more
silent, nothing-to-say-for-herself young woman than
Angela Fairfax!

Sir Timothy Clives, a neighbour and fellow dab-
bler in debauchery who lived just over the way at
Windy Grange, had agreed to help buffet him from the
expected onslaught of foolish devices employed by
schoolroom misses to attach a man, by lending his
presence to the party. But it appeared that Sir Timothy's protection wasn't needed. Miss Fairfax didn't
seem to have either the ambition or the wit to flirt.
Nonetheless, Sydney appreciated Tim's company, for
his rational conversation would probably save him
from utter madness in the coming days.

Angela Fairfax certainly was nothing like her father. Grey, portly, ruddy-faced Lord Amesbury had
talked and laughed and flirted with Lady Brynne since
the moment he'd set foot in the Abbey. Lord Amesbury had once been smitten with Sydney's mother
during her London Season of 1779, but he'd lost her

to Sydney's father, the commanding, charismatic Julian St. James.

Having met Lord Amesbury lately during a visit to a mutual friend, the dowager had wasted no time in inviting him and his daughter up to Cumberland for some elegant rustication. Watching his petite mother now as she laughed at one of the jolly baron's jokes, Sydney wondered if this time she'd initiated the party as much for her benefit as for his. That would certainly be remarkable, and even welcome, since the dowager had not looked twice at another man since his father's death. He knew she was sometimes quite lonely.

The dearth of conversation at his end of the table, with the silent Angela Fairfax on one side and his preoccupied mother on the other, was sending Sydney into a hazy daydream, the contents of which included his horse, a stretch of deserted road beneath the shadow of Mount Blencathra, a dishevelled, buxom lass with Titian hair clasping his waist and a large jug of buttered beer.

"Harrumph!"

"Yes, Lawrence, what is it?" prompted Sydney rather sharply, having been stirred from his daydream at a poignant moment.

"Begging your pardon, m'lord," intoned the butler, his usual lofty mien replaced by a pained expression. "There's a matter requiring your immediate attention!"

A high-pitched wail, not unlike the indignant cry of a cat whose tail has been trod upon, could be plainly heard through the door, which stood slightly ajar.

"What the deuce is that!" exclaimed Sydney, followed by a firm admonition of "Down, Zeus!" to the black creature who'd emerged from beneath the table and was standing alert, his wolflike ears at attention.

"Well, m'lord, it's..."

"It's a baby's cry!" declared Miss Fairfax, abruptly getting up from the table. She stepped forward and pushed open the door. "Where did it come from?"

Staggering from surprise at Miss Fairfax's spontaneous outburst, having had to wrench a mere "yes" or "no" out of her all afternoon, Sydney followed her into the hall and stood with his guests and a number of his own servants, staring down at a reed basket. The basket appeared to contain a bundle of rags, two tiny, flailing fists and a round pink face whence the horrid noise continued to issue forth with resonance.

"It's raining buckets!" observed Sir Timothy, a slender young man with light brown hair and lively hazel eyes. "Who'd take a baby out in weather like this?"

"I answered the door, m'lord," explained Lawrence in a very loud voice to be heard above the din. "There were three raps and nothing more. I couldn't imagine who would be visiting at this time and during such a downpour. You can well imagine my surprise when I opened the door and found this basket on the top step! I did not perceive at first that it contained a... person!"

"Did you have the area searched, Lawrence?" demanded Sydney.

"A thorough search of the grounds was conducted, m'lord, and no trace of a stranger or anything out of the ordinary was discovered."

"The poor thing must be wet and cold!" exclaimed Miss Fairfax. She bent down and dug into the rags, lifting the baby out. "The rags are wet only at the surface," she announced, leading Sydney to suppose that the person who'd brought the baby had employed an umbrella. The infant was wrapped snugly in a small blanket and wore a knitted hat pulled down over its ears. It ceased its crying during the process of extraction, hiccupping repeatedly, but after getting a good look at Miss Fairfax, cried even harder.

"It wants its mother, no doubt," remarked the dowager, cluck-clucking and peering into the infant's face with an expression of tender concern.

"Where the deuce is its mother, I'd like to know!" said Sydney feelingly. "And why the deuce did she bring it here?"

Lord Amesbury affixed a monocle to his eye and bent his jolly red face over Miss Fairfax's squalling armful and observed good-naturedly, "A noisy little baggage, eh?"

"Oh! There's a letter peeking out the side," cried the dowager, reaching down and retrieving a sealed envelope from the basket. "Perhaps it will tell us something!"

Sydney accepted the envelope with a wary expression and darted a quick look round at his servants, perceiving that most of the household had congregated in the hall. One or two of the footmen were exchanging knowing looks and Sydney knew precisely what they were thinking. Since several of his servants regularly accompanied him to London, they had no doubt made his Town exploits a subject for gossip in the servants' hall. They very likely suspected that the child might be his!

Sydney had gotten used to such generalized thinking about the behaviour of "rakes," by which name he was commonly called, but it still galled him to know that many people thought him so irresponsible. Despite his roguish ways, he always ensured that the willing damsels he took to bed were guarded against the possibility of breeding. And he never, *ever* seduced an innocent.

"You may all return to your various occupations," he coolly informed his suspicious servants. "The rest of us shall retire to the drawing-room. If you please!" he added politely, motioning the way.

The servants reluctantly withdrew, and Sydney stood to the side while his guests filed past him into the drawing-room. Zeus, who'd obediently remained in the dining room till then, pranced forward at his master's nod of consent to sniff out the source of all that suspiciously catlike noise.

Miss Fairfax walked directly to the chair nearest the fire and began to unwrap the squealing bundle, all the while crooning to the child in a low, soothing voice.

"What are you doing?" Sydney asked, as Miss Fairfax appeared to be about to undo the baby's napkin.

"He or she—I don't know which just yet!—may not be wet on the outside, but I daresay there's a distinct possibility that he or she is wet on the underside!"

"You don't mean to change the child's napkin in my drawing-room, do you?" Sydney exclaimed, incredulous.

"Do you wish to listen to this racket all night, my lord?" she asked him, proceeding with the task very efficiently.

"Well, no, but—"

"Angela, my love," blustered her father. "Let his lordship call a servant or something!"

"Oh! It's . . . I mean *he's* a boy!"

"Thank you, Miss Fairfax, for enlightening us," observed Sydney in a wry tone. If she were an angel, she was proving to be a deuced outrageous one!

"Perhaps the letter will tell us the boy's name," Sir Timothy suggested, nodding pointedly in the direction of the envelope Sydney still held in his hand.

Sydney frowned at his impatient friend, then frowned down at the envelope. He wasn't at all eager to relieve it of its contents. He eyed the rain-splattered, dog-eared paper with his own name crawled inexpertly across the front as if it were a slime-infested fungus. He knew the child wasn't his, but, considering his rakish reputation, perhaps some foolish woman thought she could convince him otherwise.

"Would you like me to read the letter, Sydney?" enquired his mother.

"No, no! I shall read it in a moment!" he returned rather sharply, then was immediately sorry he'd lost his temper. He threw his mother an apologetic glance and moved to stand below the candelabrum on the mantelshelf.

By now the baby had stopped crying. Miss Fairfax had used a dry piece of cloth from the basket to change the baby's napkin, then handed the soiled article to Sir Timothy. Shocked to discover himself in possession of such an odorous item, he quickly carried it with two fingers to the door and placed it in the keeping of a startled footman.

With its small face composed and its complexion returned to a more flattering colour, the baby was very pleasant to look at. Large, serious blue eyes looked curiously about the room. His cap was off now and his hair proved to be strawberry blond. Four front teeth (two on the bottom and two on the top) embellished his otherwise smooth gums with a bit of decoration.

"He's a handsome little fellow, ain't he?" commended Lord Amesbury, leaning over and chucking the baby under the chin with a fat finger.

"Don't take a fancy to him," Sydney advised him, ripping open the envelope with a decisive tug. "He doesn't belong here and he'll not be staying!"

Silence reigned while Sydney read the letter to himself. The hand was very rough and the expressions typical of the servant class of people residing in the northern regions of the Lake District. Presently he sighed and lifted his eyes from the paper to rest them unseeing on the fire which danced and jumped on the grate.

"Well, what does it say?" prompted Miss Fairfax. Sydney looked up to meet the straightforward gaze of his angelic houseguest. Her soft grey eyes were alight with curiosity. And did he detect a hint of accusation lurking there as well, or did her obvious innocence merely make him feel guilty for something he had not done? Surely such a naïve chit as Miss Fairfax could not suspect him of fathering the whelp! Goaded, he handed the letter to Tim. "Here, Tim. Read it aloud!"

Sir Timothy took the letter thrust at him by Sydney, but seemed hesitant to do as he was bade. "But, Syd," he hissed beneath his breath. "Mean to say, are you sure?"

"Don't be absurd!" Sydney retorted, appalled to discover that Tim suspected him, too. "You don't really imagine that I'm in any way related to this child, do you?"

While his friend appeared to be racking his brain for a safe reply, Miss Fairfax cried impatiently, "For heaven's sake, Sir Timothy, won't you please read the thing?"

Sydney raised a brow and eyed Miss Fairfax with ever-increasing surprise. The silent, shrinking flower at his dining-table appeared to be gone forever. But her excited exclamation had done the trick. Tim set himself immediately to the task of reading.

"The letter is addressed to his lordship, the Marquess of Brynne, of course, though it *is* misspelled," began Sir Timothy. "In fact, all this is misspelled!"

"Do your best, Tim," said Sydney wearily.

"I'll abridge," he announced. "In essence it says, 'My lord, I'm leaving my treasure with you. Harry is the light of my life, but I don't have no way to care for him. Born on the wrong side of the blanket, there's no hope for him unless you take care of him. I know your kind heart!' That's it!"

"It isn't signed?" the dowager enquired.

"Of course it isn't signed, Mama," Sydney replied, exasperated. "I'm quite sure I wouldn't recognize the signature even if it were! I've probably never set eyes on its mother, much less—"

"Sydney, I never meant to imply anything of the sort," said his mother, indignant.

"Please don't call him an 'it,' my lord," Miss Fairfax reminded him. "And possibly you have met his mother. She referred to your 'kind heart' in a very familiar way!"

"I daresay she was hoping I'd have a kind heart! Or perhaps a bad memory!"

"Tsk, tsk, Sydney," Lady Brynne admonished fretfully, darting a troubled look at Miss Fairfax. "People all about the county know what a good, kindhearted man you are, a fair master, an honest and active landlord, a devoted father to little Wellesley—"

"Wellesley isn't little any longer, Mama. They accept only strapping boys at Eton!" interrupted Sydney, impatient with his mother's blatant attempts to impress Miss Fairfax. "And, please, don't persist in listing my supposed virtues in that way or I shall begin to imagine myself at my own funeral, listening to a eulogy!"

"Sydney!" scolded his mother, rapping his arm with her fan.

"The young woman is obviously uneducated," Sir Timothy observed, still holding the letter and looking it over very closely. "And perhaps she hasn't any family to help her. She was probably telling the truth when she said she had no way to care for the child. An under-servant hereabouts, perhaps."

"Poor girl," murmured Miss Fairfax.

"But what does she expect me to do about it?" asked Sydney, raising his hands and eyes to the ceiling as if he were consulting some mystical source.

"I think it very clear what she wishes you to do," Miss Fairfax stated firmly. "She wants you to take care of her child, since she finds herself unable to."

"But why me?"

Miss Fairfax shrugged. "Perhaps it is as your mother said, because you have a good reputation." Sir Timothy made a choking sound at this comment, and Miss Fairfax added, "You have a good reputation hereabouts, at least."

This comment caused everyone to look at her rather keenly and wonder how such an innocent could possibly know anything about Lord Brynne's rather different London reputation.

"Or perhaps," she continued, untroubled by their stares, "it's simply because it's quite obvious that you

have the means to assume the care of an additional
child!"

"It does not follow that I'm compelled to raise ev-
erybody's child just because I'm—"

"'Plump in the pocket' I believe is the going expression," Lord Amesbury supplied helpfully.

"What will you do with him, then?" asked Miss
Fairfax, looking down at the child. Sydney looked at
the baby, too. Harry had disengaged one chubby foot
from the folds of the blanket and was dexterously
sucking on his toes.

"There are charitable institutions for abandoned
and orphaned children," he said at last, feeling a trifle defensive. "I should know. I contribute to them
regularly!"

"And they are well and good for children who cannot do better," Miss Fairfax said, her grey eyes grown
suddenly dark as thunderclouds. "But this child has
a mother, and I think you ought to try to locate her
before you put her baby in a foundling home! If she
knew you weren't going to keep him, I'm sure she'd
want him back. Besides, I think it would be best if the
mother were helped somehow so that she could keep
little Harry. She must be suffering tremendously, my
lord!"

Suddenly it appeared that those stormy eyes had
produced a few sprinkles. Indeed, a shimmer of tears
pooled at the corners, threatening to spill over at the
first blink. She looked down at Harry again, perhaps
to hide her emotions. A bit shaken, Sydney also

looked at Harry and was forcefully reminded of
Wellesley when he was a baby.

Wellesley had been without a mother these past two
years, and despite all the love he could give him, Sydney knew that his son had missed that special tenderness only a mother could supply. Those first few
months after Caroline's death he'd thought to remarry for the child's sake, if for no other reason than
to give Wellesley brothers and sisters. But no one had
caught Sydney's fancy, much less his heart. Since then,
he'd engaged in fleeting relationships with women who
did not demand his heart, for it seemed he could not
give them even a piece of it. Indeed, he began to suspect that that particular life-sustaining organ had been
entombed with his wife.

"Well, Sydney, what do you propose to do?" asked
his mother, jerking him away from his sober thoughts.

"Yes, Sydney. What's to do?" added Sir Timothy.

Sydney stepped forward and reached a forefinger
towards one of Harry's wildly flailing fists. As the
child grabbed hold, Zeus jealously whined his objection from the braided rug by the fire.

"He's a bonny lad..." said Sydney musingly.

"If he were as homely as a mud pie, my lord," Miss
Fairfax declared with feeling, "he should engage our
tenderest sympathy equally as much!"

Despite himself, and a vague feeling of ill usage at
the hand of Harry's absent mother, Sydney was stirred
by Miss Fairfax's words, and not less so by the ardent
flush of conviction which rendered her countenance so
radiant.

"A point well taken, Miss Fairfax," he conceded, jerking his eyes away from the lady's lovely face and repossessing his finger from Harry. He moved to stand with his back to the fire, where he was greeted by a humble Zeus who prostrated himself, then rolled over on his back with his legs up in the air.

"Try for a little restraint and dignity, Zeus," Sydney admonished, but still stooped and obligingly stroked the large dog's stomach. With his face averted, he said, "We shall try to find its... rather, *Harry's* mother." When Sydney looked up, Miss Fairfax was smiling. The simple curving of her shapely lips transformed her expression into something celestial. He could almost detect a halo!

Displeased at himself for conjuring up such whimsical images, he gruffly added, "I shudder to think what this will do to my reputation... hereabouts!"

"Why don't you simply tell people from the start that Harry isn't yours?" she suggested ingenuously. "I've found that I believe people much more readily if they speak plainly and promptly."

Surprised and charmed by her candour, he smiled crookedly and returned, "They would believe he is mine all the more! Such is the unfortunate nature of human beings, Miss Fairfax."

Miss Fairfax seemed tempted to disagree with him about the nature of human beings, since she was probably inclined to believe the general population as straightforward in their thinking as she was. But Lord Amesbury looked nearly apoplectic at what she'd said already, and so she clamped her lips tightly together and stilled her tongue, but it was with an obvious effort.

Watching her struggling with herself, Sydney began to wonder if the girl sitting in the drawing-room with an infant on her knee was indeed the same one who'd refused to speak more than a monosyllable at the dinner-table.

Then his gaze fixed on Harry. The little whelp was sporting a gummy grin the likes of which would charm the meanest harridan this side of the Thames. The others, even Tim, were bending over the child, uttering the usual inanities babies are supposed to like.

Sydney sighed. He had anticipated a tedious three weeks. But he began to suspect that it might be preferable to be bored than to be suddenly confronted with an abandoned babe and a determined angel of mercy called Angela, both of whom were too charming by half!

CHAPTER TWO

THE VIEW from Angela's window would have inspired anyone with a smidgen of romantic feeling. Castlerigg Abbey was nestled in the verdant vale of Borrowdale. Situated on a slight hill, the massive, grey stone building overlooked a wide, rocky beck which spilled beneath the graceful arch of Ashness Bridge and on to Derwentwater, a huge gemlike lake bordered by the lofty fells of Skiddaw and Blencathra.

In the aftermath of the storm, rivulets of rain meandered down the mullioned window as Angela looked through it to the breathtaking scenery beyond. They'd been served dinner early, as was the general custom in the country, and a faint glimmer of sunset yet escaped the scuttling clouds to illuminate the autumn-frocked oak and birch which dotted the countryside. The mellow golds and reds melded together into a glorious patchwork quilt of natural beauty.

She felt she could grow to love this countryside. Cumberland was so much grander than Sussex! But the colourful scene blurred as Angela recalled how she came to be at Castlerigg Abbey, and her soft mouth hardened into a stubborn line. Certainly it was a magnificent house in a beautiful setting, but she would not be married off to a stranger—a rake, at that!—just to be mistress of it! If she'd known that her father was bringing her to Castlerigg Abbey for such a purpose, she would have stayed home of a certainty.

She had always been a biddable daughter, but this time her father had gone too far! He had promised her a Season! Now it was obvious that he wanted to marry her off to Lord Brynne before she'd even had a chance to dance at Almack's, or ride in the Grand Strut at Hyde Park, or even buy a bonnet in Mayfair!

And as for Lord Brynne, his reputation had preceded him even to the small village of Finchingfield, where she resided, though her father and his mother both assumed that she was ignorant of it. In truth, it was the parson's daughter, Kate, who had told her about Lord Brynne's scandalous exploits. Kate was so fortunate as to have a cousin enjoying a Season in Town who was a faithful correspondent.

Kate was her best friend, and Angela had spent a great deal of time at the parsonage as she grew up. Angela's mother had died when she was twelve and her father was frequently away from home. Because he hardly saw her, Lord Amesbury really knew very little about his daughter. He would have been appalled to learn that the parson had allowed her to run tame in the library and that from her extensive reading she had gleaned a great deal of knowledge about the world. Thus, she was intellectually much older than her eighteen years. But virginal maidens weren't expected to have the wits to fill a thimble, and that's exactly how her papa treated her.

As for little Harry, she was quite sure that the servants, and perhaps even Sir Timothy, suspected him to be the marquess's by-blow. But evidently it had still come as a surprise to everyone when she had advised Lord Brynne to deny paternity at the outset. From this she gathered that even if a young woman understood the things going on about her, it was considered indelicate to speak of them.

She, for one, believed Lord Brynne had spoken the truth when he said Harry wasn't his. There was a certain aura of integrity about his lordship which Angela hadn't expected to find in a man with his risqué reputation. Besides, the fact that he was a rake did not prejudice her against him entirely, especially since she had no intention of succumbing to his practiced charms.

However, he was still a rake, and while Angela was broad-minded enough to suppose he had good qualities despite this fact, she also knew that she could not give her heart and hand to a man incapable of being faithful. But surely they could be civil acquaintances and work together for Harry's good.

Angela let the heavy satin curtains fall back into place over the window and, moving to the high, elaborately carved and veneered Hepplewhite bed, sat down upon it. She was angry at having been duped into a trip to the Lake District, a place she had long wished to visit, only to discover that she was to be the subject of matchmaking. Yet she was beginning to regret her cool treatment of the marquess when they'd first arrived.

It was obvious that Lord Brynne was as disinclined
to be coerced into courtship as she was, and as much
a victim of a well-meaning parent as she. But just to
be sure he understood that she held no willing part in
the scheme, she'd been silent and aloof. He must have
gotten the point by now and, besides, it would be exceedingly difficult to carry on a sensible search for
Harry's mother if the two of them weren't on speaking terms.

The clock on the mantel struck seven chimes and
Angela prepared to descend to the drawing-room. She
draped an ivory-coloured Norwich shawl about her
shoulders and smoothed the skirt of her white muslin
gown. Leaving the room, she proceeded along the
gallery to the stairs, but stopped to examine the por-
traits, hung side by side, of Lord Brynne and his late
wife.

Angela thought the portrait of the handsome marquess a faithful rendering by a skilled artist. He'd
captured Lord Brynne's strong jaw, cerulean-blue eyes
and curly crop of dark chestnut hair. His eyes danced
with enthusiasm as if he felt very glad to be alive. The
marquess had changed very little since that youthful
portrait, except for the expression in his eyes. Now
they were jaded and weary.

Observing Lady Brynne's portrait, Angela imagined that the marquess's enthusiasm for life at the time
the portrait had been painted had something to do
with her. She was a handsome woman, rather than the
current notion of what was "pretty," with hair as
glossy brown as mahogany and lively brown eyes

which radiated intelligence and humour. Angela had observed how bored the marquess seemed now, and even a little melancholy when he thought himself unobserved. All day he'd exuded a kind of charming but passionless ennui. That is, until Harry arrived on the scene. That event livened him up considerably, though perhaps it was nine parts annoyance!

Angela smiled as she remembered the marquess's harried expression when he'd agreed to try to find the baby's mother. But she'd seen tenderness reflected in his eyes, too, when he'd looked at Harry. Slightly puzzled, Angela stared into the late Lady Brynne's painted face, trying to discern a trace of sadness behind the happy expression. Perhaps the marquess had truly loved his wife and that fact had made up for his philandering ways. Such could never be the case for Angela! She must be the only woman in her husband's life. It was unfashionable to expect fidelity, she knew, but she could not tolerate anything less in a marriage.

Probably she had lingered too long in her bedchamber and in the gallery, for when Angela arrived in the drawing-room all were present. The three gentlemen stood over the dowager, who appeared to be displaying a piece of stitchery for their opinion. She noticed that though Lord Brynne was not above average in height, his form was nonetheless quite imposing. He had a slim, athletic figure which showed to advantage in the sleek black evening jacket and knee-breeches. Unexpectedly, a quiver of excitement ran down her spine at the sight of him. Calming herself, she reasoned that all rakes had a little charm or else they wouldn't be successful in their sport.

Perceiving Angela's entrance, the dowager, dressed in a delicate Indian muslin of deep jade which set off her blond hair nicely, glided over and slipped her thin arm into hers, saying, "You pour the tea, my dear. I've observed you're quite an able young woman. I should not think it would be past your powers to manage even an establishment as large as the Abbey!"

Stiffening a little at such an obvious display of matchmaking machinations, Angela merely nodded and seated herself behind the tea-tray. When the marquess sauntered over to receive his cup, Angela must have frowned because he immediately exclaimed, "Good gad, Miss Fairfax! I begin to think you have a double personality! One moment you're all animation, your tongue as quick and resilient as a fiddlestick, and the next moment you're as cold and remote as Mount Hevelyn in January!"

Angela couldn't help but smile at the marquess's effective use of simile. And why should she punish him for their parents' ambitions regarding them? "I beg your pardon, my lord. I haven't been myself today," she admitted ruefully.

"Thank God!" he replied, his blue eyes twinkling. Angela found she could not help but respond to such infectious humour and returned his smile twinkle for twinkle.

"And how do you suppose little Harry goes on with his new nursery maid, Miss Fairfax?" he continued presently, obviously more resigned to Harry's indefinite stay at Castlerigg Abbey than earlier. In fact his whole manner had changed. Gone was the passionless ennui. He seemed positively interested in everything going on about him.

Angela was busy supplying Sir Timothy with a dollop of cream when she replied, "I don't know, my lord. But I imagine you can enlighten me!"

"Yes, indeed," he replied. "My housekeeper chose Fran, one of the scullery maids, to do the job. Says Fran's from a large family and knows how to go about caring for a baby. Harry took right to her, as well! They're both ensconced in Wellesley's old rooms with every comfort. Do you approve?"

Angela wasn't about to approve someone she hadn't met and was ready to say so when the marquess continued. "Knew you'd want to meet the girl. I've sent for her to come down and bring Harry with her so you can see how well they deal together. Satisfied?"

"For the present," she replied, lifting her brows and nodding in an expression of friendly challenge.

"I'll have no leniency from you, shall I?" he replied playfully, then sobered and fixed her with a penetrating eye. "In truth, short of taking the little fellow to my bosom, what *do* you expect me to do with him if his mother chooses to remain anonymous?"

"Let's not consider that as a possibility just yet," Angela replied. "I believe she's out there watching, seeing how we get on. We shall find her."

Lord Brynne raised a dubious brow, but only said, "Do you think so? Well, at any rate, I propose we be-

gin the enquiries at the George and Vulture at Rosethwaite, our closest village. Ebeneezer Cooper, the
innkeeper there, knows the comings and goings of any
and all that pass through the valley.''

"And he ought to know if some local farmer's
daughter has been, er, with child in the past year,''
added Sir Timothy, who moved to stand next to the
marquess. "Weeping into his heavy wet, many a man's
spilled his troubles in old Ebeneezer's taproom!''

"Don't suppose it's one of your tenant's children,
do you, Brynne?'' suggested her father, his florid
complexion deepened by too much after-dinner port.

"I know my tenants quite well,'' replied the marquess. "And I don't think that's possible. But it won't
hurt to make enquiries. I'll set my steward to it first
thing in the morning, have him call at all the cottages
and so on. And just so we don't bore ourselves silly in
this process of finding Harry's mother, we'll mix
pleasure with business tomorrow and visit Castlerigg
Circle after we've done our duty at the George. Rather
an impressive spectacle, that. What do you say, Miss
Fairfax?''

"That would be delightful,'' Angela replied
brightly. She had heard of the Circle, rumoured to
have been the haunt of Druids in ancient times. She
had a fetish for ruins and couldn't wait to see this one.

"Oh, and here's our little poppet!'' cooed the dowager as Lawrence opened the door to admit the scullery maid, Fran, holding a beaming, drooling Harry.
Close behind them loped Zeus, drooling as well.

"Fran, I'd like you to meet some of Harry's well-wishers," said the marquess, treating the maid as politely as if she'd been presented at Court with the best of them. "They wanted to, er, see you, m'dear."

After the short, apple-cheeked maid had completed several curtsies—no easy task with Harry in tow—and gently pried a strand of her long blond hair from Harry's wet, tenacious fingers, she replied, "It's right you are t'see who the little feller's got to watch over 'im. He's a right luvly lad, he is!"

"I couldn't agree with you more," said Angela, smiling warmly at the young girl, who she guessed to be no more than sixteen. "Are you sure you can carry him properly, Fran, without straining your back? He's nearly as big as you are!"

"I'll manage, miss! Tickles me pink t'take care of 'im." Then, as if to prove it, Fran did turn pink, and said, "Gets me out o' the kitchen, you know!"

"How long have you been in my employ, Fran?" asked the marquess.

"Since the first of June, m'lord."

"Only that long, eh? Well, Mrs. Mumford tells me you have several brothers and sisters," he said. "Drawing on your vast experience, can you tell us how old Harry is?"

Fran pondered for a minute, wrinkling her freckled nose and nearly crossing her eyes with the effort. "His teeth are breakin' through 'is gums. I'd say he's four or five months."

"Thank you, Fran. That's helpful information."

Fran shrugged and dug her heel into the carpet, accidently stepping on Zeus's tail, which was fanned luxuriously directly in front of her. Zeus scurried to his feet and sat on his haunches next to Fran, stoically suppressing a yelp.

"Lor', Zeus! I didn't see you there!" she apologized. "He's been followin' me ever since I took over carin' fer little Harry."

"How noble of you, Zeus," the marquess observed dryly, bending forward to address the dog. "Have we assigned ourselves the task of protecting the little fellow?" Zeus flattened his ears and showed his teeth in a wide, lolling dog smile.

Angela laughed and began to suspect that Lord Brynne was not an ordinary rake, or, indeed, an ordinary peer of the realm. A marquess who talked in a friendly manner to dogs and scullery maids was definitely unusual!

SYDNEY SUMMONED HIS LAND steward to his library first thing the following morning and enquired briefly about his crops, his stock and his tenants. According to the steward, Mr. Ned Holmes, all were in fine fettle, as far as he knew.

"Have you been round to see all the tenants lately, Mr. Holmes?" asked Sydney, coming at last to the point of the meeting. "Please don't think I'm questioning the performance of your duties. I know you're an excellent steward, or you wouldn't be working for me. But I've an especial reason for asking."

Mr. Holmes, a well-grown, good-looking young man with weather-roughened skin and of a phlegmatic nature, said, "No. Can't say that I have, m'lord. Too many other things to do with the harvesting to finish up and the barns and stables to secure for the winter coming on."

"Perfectly understandable, Mr. Holmes. But I hope you find yourself a little more at leisure this week, because I should like you to visit all the tenants. I've a particular task for you to accomplish, one which might require all your powers of subtlety and tact."

If this statement intrigued Mr. Holmes, he did not indicate as much by any change of expression. In his usual taciturn fashion, he merely waited for the marquess to continue.

"You may have heard... These kinds of things are generally impossible to keep quiet about the estate! A baby was left on the doorstep yesterday afternoon and I've a mind to discover if the mother is someone nearby, starting with my tenants. It's very unlikely that the, er, perpetrator will come right out and tell you the baby is hers, so you will no doubt have to resort to roundaboutation! Do you catch my meaning?"

"Yes, m'lord," replied Mr. Holmes.

"Good! How soon might I expect you to report back?"

"By tomorrow morning I should have seen them all, sir."

"I shall talk to you then. I'm off to Rosethwaite to see old Ebeneezer at the George today. How are the roads?"

"Better than I'd thought to see 'em, m'lord. Sun's been shining strong all morning and there's a westerly wind. Passable."

"Even for a barouche?"

"By early afternoon, m'lord, I expect so."

"Thank you, Mr. Holmes." Sydney dismissed his steward with a handshake and a smile. The young man had proven himself an excellent manager in the two years since the marquess had hired him on the recommendation of his last steward, who'd grown too old to ride the snow-covered fells in the course of his winter duties. Despite the steward's reticent nature, Sydney had perfect faith in Mr. Holmes's ability to pry information out of his tenants, as well as give him an accurate assessment of the roads.

"Sydney! Still got your nose to the grindstone, I see!" exclaimed Sir Timothy, sauntering into the room with his thumbs hooked in the pockets of his white pantaloons.

"You're up early," Sydney commented wryly, flicking his friend a quick glance, then returning his gaze to the letter he was reading.

Sir Timothy dropped into a chair, leaned back and crossed his legs at the ankle. Then he lifted his arms above his head and twined his fingers together behind his neck in an attitude of complete relaxation. "There is really no point in one lying abed when one is compelled to retire the night before at eleven o'clock, is there?" he drawled. "Perhaps if I'd had a companion to share my bed this morning, I might have been persuaded to, er, *repose* a little longer, but as it is . . ."

"You knew how it would be when I invited you, Tim," the marquess reminded him calmly, never lifting his eyes from the letter. "This was not to be the same style of house party you have enjoyed at my London residence. But if you are regretting your decision to bear me company through this particular house party, I shall understand if you leave."

Tim sat up, leaned his elbows on his knees and clasped his hands loosely together. "Odd thing is, I don't want to leave, Syd," he confessed, a puzzled frown creasing his forehead. "I must admit that at dinner yesterday I was cudgelling my brain for some reason to excuse myself from the Abbey." He grinned sheepishly. "But then Harry arrived on the scene and livened things up a bit."

Sydney raised a disbelieving brow. "Indeed, Tim, I had no notion you were so fond of children."

"I like them well enough," admitted Tim, "but it isn't Harry who's keeping me at the Abbey, though I'll admit he's a taking little scamp and I've an interest in the outcome of the mystery attached to him."

"Then what . . . ?"

Tim leaned forward in his chair. "Did you not notice how very much the shrinking violet blossomed after Harry came? Begad, she's an angel, ain't she?"

Sydney pursed his lips. "I take it you are referring to Miss Fairfax?"

"Who else?" retorted Tim, laughing. "I was struck by her beauty immediately, but until she spoke and revealed how very lively, intelligent and passionate she is . . ."

"Passionate?" repeated the marquess, frowning.

"In good works she is passionate," explained Tim. "Indeed, she stood up for Harry and his unfortunate mother with all the zeal of a Methodist! Such passion in one area promises a corresponding degree of passion in other areas, as well."

"An interesting theory, Tim, but hardly useful in this case," Sydney replied dampeningly. "Miss Fairfax is a respectable young woman. What passions lie within her virginal breast will be discovered by her husband and no other."

"Good gad, what a sober-sides you are!" declared Tim, laughing. "Aren't you even tempted to get up a flirtation with the chit? Might alleviate some of the boredom you're bound to endure over the next three weeks!"

"Tim, I'm surprised at you," Sydney returned with a small smile. "I am not accustomed to pursuing innocents in an effort to relieve boredom. Nor am I willing to risk losing my freedom because I have compromised some schoolroom miss. The pleasure would be fleeting and hardly worth the consequences. Besides, seducing virgins is a bit cruel, don't you think?"

"Zounds, Syd!" Tim exclaimed, offended. "Did you suppose I meant . . . ? Indeed, I was only suggesting you ought to steal a kiss from the girl, not ravage her!"

"I am loath to remind you of it, my friend," persisted the marquess with patient good humour, "but you should know the dangers and discomforts attached to toying with green girls. When dealing with

respectable women, even a kiss can precipitate a betrothal. I don't think you realize how close you were
to parson's mousetrap after that incident at the Pembertons' lawn party. Vicar Beakman has never forgiven you for taking his daughter down to the boat-
house!''

"And the worst of it is, I don't even remember what
happened!" complained Tim. "Too jug-bit by half! I
don't even recall how we got to the boat-house, much
less what happened after we got there!''

"She told her father that you'd merely kissed her,"
said Sydney, "which, I should hope, was all you could
do in the short time you were there. But if her father
hadn't sought her out when he did, I shudder to think
what might have happened! I'm awfully glad you
nipped that drinking habit in the bud, Tim. Entirely
losing one's memory when one is foxed is a sure indi-
cation that one ought not to drink!''

"Deuced pretty girl!" mumbled Tim, frowning.
"Always thought she was pretty, but too reserved for
my tastes. Don't know how I managed even to talk her
into going with me to the boat-house!" Tim suddenly
looked horrified. "Begad, I hope I didn't *drag* her
there!''

"I daresay she went willingly enough," opined
Sydney. "But innocents are particularly dangerous
when they're willing! Daresay the vicar didn't insist
you marry the chit because he doesn't like you above
half, Tim. Even your fortune could not tempt the
prodigiously good vicar to overlook your blemished
character!''

"Haven't seen Miss Beakman in an age," Tim observed pensively, completely oblivious of Sydney's teasing thrust.

"Still visiting her aunt in Portsmouth, no doubt," supplied Sydney, eyeing his friend curiously. "Are you smitten with the girl, Tim? You needn't follow my example and remain a bachelor the rest of your days, you know. Marriage can be wonderful, if you're lucky, as I was with Caroline. But I cannot hope to duplicate such happiness, such magic, again. I feel I shall be much safer and much less disappointed if I remain in a single state. You, however..."

"Told you, Syd. Miss Beakman's too reserved for me!" Tim stated flatly, then promptly changed the subject. "When are we off to the George? Getting a little restless!"

"I'm almost done here. Why don't you go and find the newly blossomed Miss Fairfax and amuse yourself till I'm through?" the marquess suggested dryly.

"You mock me, Syd, but unless I've gone queer in the attic, you find the chit amusing, too! You were ready to nod off at dinner, but once Harry came and Miss Fairfax shook off her shyness, you positively perked up!"

"One can find an innocent amusing, can't one?" the marquess coolly defended himself. "Especially when she is as fresh and free-spoken as Miss Fairfax. It does not mean, however, that I've any intention to bed *or* wed the chit."

"Beware, Syd," taunted his friend. "Your words just now smack of admiration!"

"Be off with you, Tim, before I take a notion to draw your cork!" warned the marquess with a grim smile.

Tim emitted a loud guffaw and left the room and the marquess to his estate business.

ANGELA WAITED in the drawing-room along with the others for Lord Brynne to join them. A little past noon he strolled in, cutting a dashing figure in his buff breeches, Wellington boots, black waistcoat and forest green jacket.

Suddenly Angela was glad she had taken the trouble to select an especially pretty walking dress of blush-coloured sarsenet and a matching bonnet in the new cottage shape made of blush-coloured lutestring. Her light pelisse was dove-coloured lutestring, trimmed in ermine. After all, she reasoned, it would not do for the marquess to think that just because she was from a small village in Sussex, she was not up to snuff!

The morning sun had dried up the roads a trifle and they were now on their way only little bogged down by the remnants of yesterday's storm. Angela could not have cared a fig about the inconvenience of a little dirt and smiled happily as they bumped and jolted along the lane to Rosethwaite in Lord Brynne's comfortable barouche. She found herself facing forward and settled between the two gentlemen, while her father and the tiny dowager were paired and sitting opposite. Zeus, who now seemed to divide his time between Harry and Lord Brynne, was balancing his hefty weight on the floor between them.

The conversation, which the gentlemen took upon themselves to monopolize, was kept to the weather and politics. When Angela ventured a strong opinion about the continuing difficulty of finding honest employment for the men who had fought the war against Napoleon and were now, in many cases, impoverished, she thought she perceived a look of astonishment on the faces of both Lord Brynne and Sir Timothy. She sighed inwardly, sorry to be shown yet another example of patent disbelief by the male population in the existence of rational thought in virginal maidens.

Presently they reached the village of Rosethwaite, its reed-thatched cottages weathered to a grey opalescent lustre. They turned in at the small courtyard belonging to the George and Vulture, which was a modest, clean establishment and appeared to be run by quite an affable innkeeper. The marquess bespoke a private parlour and Mr. Cooper showed the party of swells into his best room with cordial deference.

After ordering a light collation, the marquess and Sir Timothy excused themselves to visit the taproom for a private word with "Old Eb." But in his haste to exit the room, the marquess left his faithful companion behind. Zeus looked stricken for a moment, then moved to the window facing the back of the inn and looked dejectedly through its open casement.

"B'God, I'm hungry!" exclaimed Lord Amesbury a few moments later as a maid came in and began setting the table with heavy pewter dishes and glassware. "I hope the marquess's enquiries don't take much longer. I daresay it would be rude to eat without them, eh, my little dumpl—'' The earl caught himself before the endearment had completely passed his lips and slid a guilty look at Angela.

Angela endeavoured to appear as vacant-minded as her fond parent hoped, and pretended she hadn't heard. For some reason her father thought it indelicate to reveal to his daughter that Lady Brynne was his *chère amie,* but in her opinion no two people could appear more obviously besotted with each other. She wondered why they didn't simply marry and have done with it.

''My Lord Amesbury,'' tittered the dowager, a little fretful about the earl's *faux pas,* ''Sydney and Sir Timothy are bound to return at any moment....''

Suddenly Zeus let out a low, menacing growl. They all looked over towards the window and saw the animal poised, body stiff, tail sticking straight out and ears erect.

''What's the matter, Zeus? What do you see?'' Angela called out, rising from her chair to cross the room. But just as she reached the window, Zeus lifted his snout to the ceiling and howled. Apparently this was some sort of canine bugle call, signalling his intention to charge. Squeezing his large body through the half-opened window, Zeus was off across the wooded field behind the inn with a vengeance. And if she did not err, Angela thought she saw a dark figure disappear behind the trees!

''Hmm... How very odd!'' muttered Angela to herself. Zeus had seemed to her quite a friendly dog.

Who might he have taken such a strong dislike to at first sight? Then, much intrigued, she determined to find out why Zeus found the fleeing person so objectionable. But as she pushed a chair under the window-sill, her father cried out, "Angela, child! What *are* you doing?"

"Don't worry, Papa, I'll be back!" she assured him, then slid onto the window ledge and dropped herself carefully to the ground.

"Go after her, Percy. Indeed, my dear, this is not *seemly!*" shrieked the dowager, as they watched Angela sprint towards the woods.

"I'd never catch up with her, sweeting! She runs like a gazelle! And I'd be bound to fall into a spasm if I tried!"

"Oh, *that* would never do!" agreed the dowager. "I'll fetch Sydney!"

Angela soon discovered that the ground was much damper than it appeared. Her pattens sank into the soft earth with each step. She'd taken off her pelisse and bonnet in the parlour and was therefore relieved of the extra weight and bother, but her narrow skirt did not permit her to run very fast. Zeus was entirely out of sight now in the thick knot of trees, but she could hear him barking.

Presently the woods thinned out and a clearing was visible through the trees. Angela stopped at the edge of the clearing to catch her breath and saw Zeus several yards ahead. He was climbing a gentle rise of hill distinguished by a group of large upright stones. No doubt this was Castlerigg Circle, the Druid ruins they

planned to visit that very afternoon! Then a flash of
dark cloth caught her eye and she was sure she saw
someone dart behind one of the stones.

Seizing hold of her skirt, she pulled the hem up to
the middle of her calves and ran as fast as she could.
But when she reached the circle, Zeus was running
back and forth between the stones and barking as if
he'd lost his quarry. Angela was quite out of breath by
now and leaned against one of the stones, clutching
her side.

She looked from one stone to the next—each of
them so perfectly spaced from the other—and saw
nothing. In and about the circle there was complete
stillness. She marvelled that anyone could have out-
run Zeus and reached the wooded copse on the opposite side of the circle to get completely away. And
why would someone go to so much trouble to avoid
being seen?

"Miss Fairfax?"

Much to her credit, Angela did not shriek. Indeed,
since her heart had leapt into her throat, it was impossible at first to utter a sound.

"Lord Brynne, it's you!" she breathed thankfully,
when she observed his slim, straight form behind her.

"And whom, pray tell, were you expecting?" he
enquired, amusement writ in every feature.

CHAPTER THREE

"I DON'T KNOW, exactly," Angela admitted, a trifle irritated by the marquess's obvious amusement. "I didn't see him!"

"You didn't see *whom,* Miss Fairfax?"

"The man that Zeus was chasing, of course!"

Lord Brynne's brows drew together. "Zeus was chasing a man?" he repeated doubtfully. "Don't you know, Miss Fairfax, that the epithet 'man's best friend' was penned with dogs like Zeus in mind? He's much too amiable to take objection to anyone but the devil himself!"

"Well, that is why I found it so interesting that he was chasing someone," explained Angela with a slight lift of her chin. "I thought he must have a good reason for it!"

"But where is this person?" he asked her, raising a hand and indicating the area with an all-encompassing gesture. "If, as you say, you didn't see him, how do you know *what* Zeus was chasing?"

"But I did see him, in a way, I suppose..." she said, beginning to feel foolish. Zeus was still zigzagging back and forth between the stones, his nose pressed to the ground. "Well then, if you don't think Zeus was chasing someone, why is he so agitated?'' she demanded to know.

The marquess raised a supercilious brow. "Zeus's starts are quite nonsensical, Miss Fairfax. It's anybody's guess why he took to the chase this afternoon.'' He looked over at his dog and observed him for a full minute before saying, "He *is* rather excited, though. My guess is he saw a fox. Wish *I* had!''

Angela sighed lustily, at the same time blowing a wisp of hair out of her eyes. "You think just as men always do, Lord Brynne,'' she accused him warmly. "Just like Papa, you don't credit me with having a bit of common sense! My instincts are quite good! After Harry's appearance on your doorstep last night, I should think you'd allow the possibility of some sort of skullduggery going on round here!''

"Well, my dear,'' he conceded in what Angela construed as a rather patronizing tone, "I can't help but think like a man, since, though you may not have noticed it, I do belong to that particular gender—''

Indeed she had noticed . . . drat the man!

"—but my thoughts, whether influenced by my gender or not, lead me to wonder whether this person was running simply because a large black dog was in hot pursuit. If one is not acquainted with Zeus, one might think him rather ferocious.''

"But you said yourself that Zeus does not generally take a dislike to anybody!''

"True. So possibly there is something in what you say. But do you always act upon your instincts in such an energetic fashion? Why didn't you come and fetch *me* to chase this person down?"

Lord Brynne was standing not an arm's length away. Looking up into his blue eyes, Angela felt herself strangely beguiled by the mix of amusement and understanding reflected there. Then, when his eyes dropped below her neck for a rather keen perusal of her person, she realized what a sight she must have been! Her pattens were ankle-high in mud, a sleeve was torn on her lovely walking dress, and her hair was loosed from its combs and flying like a wild spiderweb about her face. She must have looked an absolute fright!

"There was no time to fetch you, my lord," she said, then added wryly, "I suppose you're looking at me like that because, in addition to everything else, I've a large blob of mud on my nose!"

The marquess did not answer at first. He merely watched her with that same keen glint in his eye. Soon she imagined his gaze was like a magnifying glass, collecting and centring the heat of the sun, for she felt her skin warm beneath its intensity.

"No, your nose is as clean and as charming as ever," he said at last in a low voice. "But you do have a spot, just *there*...." He lifted his hand and cupped her chin, wiping the soft indentation below her parted lips with a slow stroke of his thumb.

Angela was speechless. His hand was so warm and sure, the stroke of his thumb so...*agreeable* that her breath caught in her throat and goose bumps erupted all over her. Then, suddenly, his hand dropped. "You *are* a sight, though," he informed her in his former light-hearted manner.

Chastising herself for reacting in such an idiotic and shockingly *physical* way to the marquess's simple, friendly gesture, Angela bracingly agreed, "Yes, I suppose I am! And I did run off rather impetuously. But I am certain Zeus saw someone he took a strenuous objection to...."

"For no apparent reason," the marquess pointed out.

"For a reason we'll perhaps understand by and by, Lord Brynne!"

"Well, we shall see about that, but in the meantime I propose we return to the inn before your father and my mother are beside themselves with worry! No doubt you shall wish to tidy up a bit before luncheon. Where's Zeus?"

Lord Brynne turned to face the circle and was caught off guard by Zeus, who loped across the ground at a fast pace, jumped up and placed his large, muddy paws on the marquess's chest. A weaker man might have toppled over from the unexpected force of such an affectionate attack, but his lordship was only compelled to take a step or two backwards.

"Good God, Zeus!" he exclaimed. "Look what you've done to my jacket, you ramshackle cur!"

Observing the two muddy paw prints on the marquess's impeccable lapels, quite distinctly outlined against the pristine green of his elegant jacket, Angela could not refrain from laughing. "Now we're on a more equal footing, Lord Brynne," she informed him as he grimly eyed his jacket, then his dog, who'd flattened his ears and dropped his tail in a show of abject repentance.

Finally the marquess looked over at her and she was pleased to see the self-effacing grin on his face. "Yes, now neither of us is fit to be seen! Watch your step," he advised as he took her arm in his and began to retrace their steps back to the George. "Any further mishap to your lovely dress would be a shame!"

"Tell me about the Circle, my lord," Angela suggested, hoping to divert her mind from the return of those dreadful goose bumps, apparently caused by her closeness to the marquess.

"It's called Castlerigg Circle, you know," he began, seeming quite at his ease. "A portion of the estate meanders this way, and I suppose, by law, it belongs to me. But I'm of the opinion that all sites of historical significance, like the circles found all round England, belong to the public."

He stopped and pointed towards Mount Blencathra. "Looking down at the Circle from up there, you can see the perfect regularity of the stones—thirty-eight altogether. And the ten stones in the middle are equally well spaced. An imaginary line drawn through the centre of the circle, pointing northeast to Fiends' Fell—yes, a colourful name, isn't it?—passes through another circle near Penrith, just like this one, called Long Meg and her Daughters."

"How fascinating!"

"And the line which passes through the circle, Miss Fairfax, is the precise direction of sunrise on the first day of May! Can you imagine the mystical pagan ceremonies which took place on this desolate plateau each first dawn of May, year after year?''

Angela had a lively imagination and could easily conjure up an alarming vision of spellbound, scantily clad virgins dancing round a bonfire, though how closely this vision resembled the actual ceremony was extremely questionable. But the picture she'd conjured up had unaccountably warmed her blood. Perhaps, as a virgin herself, she could sense the spirits of her long-dead pagan sisters and was feeling the fire as surely as if she'd been there herself. As she glanced up at the marquess and encountered that inexplicable glint, the flames felt closer still. She was ever so relieved when she spied Sir Timothy walking up the hill to find them.

SYDNEY WAS PLEASANTLY surprised by the amount of food Mrs. Cooper had prepared for them. As sharpset as he was himself, the others seemed equally as ravenous. They polished off an entire round of cream cheese, wrapped in a clean cloth and served in a wooden bowl, a whole dressed chicken with its liver tucked under a wing and tidy parsley buttonholes on its fat bosom, white scones, fluffy and soft, which powdered the lips as the teeth sank into the salty butter in the middle, and a jar of bilberry jam.

After several cups of tea to wash it down, they were ready to set out for a more thorough perusal of the Castlerigg stones. Sydney sent the maid to the kitchen to roust Rob, the coachman, from his stool in the taproom with orders to set the horses to at his earliest convenience.

"This time we shall ride round to the Circle like civilized Englishmen . . . and ladies," he informed the others, winking at Angela.

"You haven't said whether Mr. Cooper told you anything helpful, Lord Brynne," Miss Fairfax observed, pretending not to have noticed the wink, though her blushing cheeks told all. She'd gone directly to a room to repair her dress and hair when they'd first arrived back at the inn, his mother cluck-clucking and trailing along and her father wringing his pudgy hands in concern, but she still looked a little rumpled. Her gown had been brushed and the torn shoulder seam hastily stitched by a chambermaid, but the general impression of charming disarray still hung about her lovely person. Her hair, glinting silver-gold in the late afternoon sun spilling through the window, had been brushed and pinned, but a stray wisp or two curved gently round her neck.

"Tabby got your tongue, Syd?"

Tim's insinuating voice recalled Sydney to the present. "Nothing! He'd nothing to tell me, Miss Fairfax," he said at last.

"Mr. Cooper had seen no one unusual," Tim further explained, "nor been the recipient of anyone's confidence which would lead him to suppose they are relatives of Harry's."

"Drat! What dreadful luck!" said Miss Fairfax. "What shall we do *now*?"

"It seems hopeless!" said Lady Brynne in a tone of resignation.

"Don't fret, my little, er, that is, my lady!" soothed Lord Amesbury, flushed and drowsy from the food and several tankards of ale. "There's bound to be something else we can do!"

"By tomorrow noon my steward will have visited all my tenants, Mama," said Sydney. "Perhaps he'll have dug up some information we can use to try to locate Harry's mother."

"I hope so," returned Miss Fairfax, a line of worry appearing between her brows. Lord Brynne had to stifle an urge to smooth away the line with his fingers. Since he'd touched her earlier at the Circle and felt how very supple and soft her skin was, he had rather a strong craving to touch her again! But that would not be at all wise! He had need of listening to one of his own sermons about avoiding innocents!

"Milord!"

Rob the coachman stood at the door of the parlour, which the maid had left open, his ruddy jowls tucked into the folds of his neckcloth and his chest puffed out like a pouter pigeon. Rob had had a stint in the navy and liked to imagine Lord Brynne in the role of admiral and himself a faithful recruit.

"What is it, Rob? Is the carriage ready?"

"No, sir!" he answered, with a military punch to his words. "That is, yes, sir, the carriage *is* ready. But I thought as 'ow you'd like to see what I found tucked into the squabs! It's a letter, sir, addressed to you. Since it t'weren't there afore when I put the coach and 'orses in the stable, someone must've sneaked it in whilst we was having our potables, sir!''

"There, you see!" exclaimed Miss Fairfax. "That was who Zeus was chasing! The stable yards can be clearly seen from that window!"

"Yes, so it would seem," murmured the marquess, accepting the letter from Rob with little enthusiasm.

"There's no basket containing an infant or a litter of kittens lying about, is there, Rob?" asked Tim with a grin.

"Never mind, Rob," Sydney drawled, casting his friend a dampening look. "Sir Timothy was only joking. You may go. We'll be there in a moment."

The marquess waited until Rob had closed the door behind him before saying, "Receiving my mail in this backhanded fashion is proving to be downright nerve-shattering! I can't imagine it containing *good* news, or the author would have handed it to me directly."

"Yes, indeed! Exactly my thoughts!" agreed Lord Amesbury sympathetically, striving hard to stay awake so as not to miss out on the excitement.

"Oh, do please hurry and open it!" cried Miss Fairfax.

The marquess opened the letter. The slip of paper inside contained a very short message.

"What does it say?" chirped the dowager.

"Is it written in the same hand?" Miss Fairfax demanded.

"It says, 'Leave well enough alone. Send the little by-blow to an orphanage and be done with it. Attempting to find the child's mother is a mistake. I give you fair warning.' Good God, what do you suppose they mean by that? And, no, it is not written in the same hand as the note which accompanied Harry!''

"Begad, who do you suppose wrote such a note?" exclaimed Tim.

"Perhaps a friend or relative of the mother's, or, more probably, Harry's father!" said Sydney thoughtfully, flipping the sheet of parchment against his open palm in an absent gesture.

"If Harry's father wrote such a mean-spirited note, I feel all the more sympathy for his mother!" declared Miss Fairfax. "It sounds as though he has no sense of responsibility in the matter, or, indeed, any proper feelings! We *must* find her, Lord Brynne! Who knows what difficulties she may be enduring?''

Lord Brynne couldn't help but admire Miss Fairfax's compassionate nature, but the entire matter was getting out of hand. What if he couldn't find the child's mother? What if the father, or whoever this note-writer was, became more insistent in his threats? And how on earth had he gotten himself caught up in this bumblebroth in the first place?

"Miss Fairfax, I begin to think it expedient that we contact the constable, or the vicar at the very least...."

"What can they do that you cannot? I hope you don't mean to throw the child on the Parish? They'll only put him in an orphanage till he's six or seven, then put him to work in the foundries or the pits! Even if they found him a home, being a child of the mist he's likely to be scorned, denied an education, and raised to be a labourer doing their dirtiest chores!''

"That is not always the case, Miss Fairfax. And I would take great pains to ensure that Harry did not meet with such a fate. I only thought the vicar or the constable might have some information we could use. But I must admit that I don't know what to do just yet," he marquess said with a heavy sigh. "It is to be hoped Mr. Holmes will have discovered something! In the meantime, I suggest we go back to the Abbey directly."

"Splendid idea, my lord," said Lord Amesbury, staring owlishly from beneath his sluggish eyelids.

"Yes," agreed Miss Fairfax, the line between her brows more deeply etched than before. "I've a mind to look in on Harry!"

LORD AMESBURY SLEPT soundly during the short trip back to the Abbey, his hands twined and resting on his large stomach, his mouth falling open with each sonorous snore. Angela's mind was greatly occupied with Harry's situation, but when at one point her papa's resonating wheeze fairly shook the carriage, she felt compelled to apologize for him.

"Do not trouble to apologize," Lady Brynne assured her, reaching over to pat her on the knee. "Sydney and Tim do not mind, and, indeed, your papa's snoring never disturbs *me!*"

Angela puzzled over this statement for a moment, and was about to ask the dowager how she had become so intimate with her papa's propensity to snore, when Lord Brynne drew her attention to some village children cavorting in a nearby mud hole.

Shortly the Abbey came into view. Rambling, asymmetrical, part original grey stone and the other part modern stucco, it had an eccentric magnificence about it which Angela could not help but admire. The high gothic windows reflected the golden brilliance of the late sun and seemed to beckon them home. They had crossed Ashness Bridge, entered through the lodge gates and were climbing the hill to the front courtyard when she observed a plain, black curricle and matching black geldings stationed in front of the arched and pointed entryway.

"You've callers, Syd!" exclaimed Tim. "Not the vicar, is it?"

The marquess leaned towards a window and looked out. "Yes, I'm afraid it is. I should recognize that black coach and horses anywhere. The pious Vicar Beakman is a staid fellow, Miss Fairfax, right down to that sober equipage of his. Looks like an undertaker's! And he's got a servant to drive him about who looks like a gravedigger! Lean and sallow as an iron rod, and with a perpetual pinched look about the mouth. Wonder where Joseph is today? Moralizing to my servants in the stables, perhaps. He's as bad as the vicar when it comes to belabouring the virtues of good over evil!"

"Is the vicar a relative of yours?" Angela enquired, curious.

"Distantly," admitted the marquess. "Daresay my father was feeling sorry for Beakman when he granted him the living, since he was unsuccessful in life and desperately in need of an income. He's a widower with one daughter. Found his niche in the church, though. Embraced the pulpit with a vengeance! Loves to preach. But our old vicar was much more the thing— much more effective. He knew how to inspire one to do good without cramming the church down one's throat."

"You don't suppose he's heard about Harry and has come to meddle, do you?" asked Angela, a knot of dread forming in her stomach. "What if he takes Harry away?"

"As quickly as news spreads about, Miss Fairfax, it's entirely possible he's heard about Harry. But on the other hand, he could be here to subject me to the usual sermon on morality, in the guise of a social call, he seems compelled to deliver each time I return from a polluting trip to Town! Somehow he's formed the impression that everyone's up to mischief in London!" he slyly added.

"I daresay such provincials as he haven't the slightest notion what really draws a young man like yourself to London, Sydney," said Lady Brynne, with a nervous glance at Angela. "Why, the museums alone are worth the trip! And the musical society is by far the most—"

"Doing it a bit brown, ain't you, Mama?" suggested Lord Brynne with a wink.

"Sydney!" the dowager admonished, rapping his knuckles with her fan.

When it was apparent that the teasing banter did not calm or amuse Angela, the marquess quickly assured her, "No one shall take Harry away against my wishes, Miss Fairfax. Don't fret!"

Angela was finally prodded out of her worrisome thoughts by Lord Brynne's words. She looked towards him and thought his blue eyes conveyed a great deal of confidence. She began to feel much more comfortable. Indeed, she even dared believe that the marquess's air of unruffled authority could suppress any mere clergyman's wishes concerning Harry.

She threw him a grateful smile which he acknowledged with a slight nod and a warm twinkle in his eye.

"I don't wish to see the vicar, Syd," Sir Timothy stated flatly, having up till then been as silent as Angela. "Got to contrive to get past him and up the stairs before he sees me."

"Yes, that would be best," agreed his friend. "I'll wager he'd as lief miss seeing you, too, Tim!"

"Why don't you want to see the vicar, Sir Timothy?" Angela asked him, puzzled. "It sounds as though *neither* of you like him very much!"

"It is not that we dislike him so very much, Miss Fairfax," explained the marquess dryly. "It is just that the vicar is such a prodigiously *good* man, and so vastly proud of it that he makes Tim and me feel dashed uncomfortable!"

"Sydney! You shall give Miss Fairfax a very bad idea of your character if you continue to talk so!" admonished the dowager, exasperated.

"You need not try to shelter me, my lady," Angela advised her matter-of-factly. "You and Papa ought to know by now that I have heard all about your son's reputation, and while I find it unfortunate that he has chosen a rakish style of life, it is none of *my* concern, after all. As for his general character, I shall make up my own mind about *that!*" She rested her sparkling grey eyes speculatively on the marquess. "Sometimes I think Lord Brynne wishes me to think him a worse sort of fellow than he really is! But I daresay nothing he could say would shock me. I read every sort of book, you know, and not just Fordyce's *Sermons!*"

Greatly surprised to hear such opinions coming from the mouth of an innocent, those three occupants of the carriage who were still awake finished the journey without a peep.

Indeed, Lord Brynne was more and more intrigued, despite himself. So, she was a reader, he thought, perhaps even a bit of a bluestocking, just as Caroline was. A beautiful woman with as much wit as hair was hard to come by.

Ignorant of, and therefore unperturbed by his daughter's little speech, Lord Amesbury continued to snore as loudly as ever.

The barouche came to a halt at the front of the Abbey and the carriage door was opened by a footman. Zeus jumped out and made straight for the vicar's gig, sniffing all about it like a hound on the scent, then bounded towards the stables till one of the cook's cats strolled across the drive and distracted him.

When the others disembarked and entered the Abbey, Sir Timothy made hastily for the stairs, but, as luck would have it, the vicar was standing directly in the way of Tim's escape route, accepting his hat from

Lawrence. A young woman stood beside him. Angela expected Tim to retreat, and go round and up the servants' back stairway, but the sight of Vicar Beakman and the girl beside him seemed to hold him in thrall.

Noting the arrival of the Abbey's residents, Vicar Beakman returned his hat to Lawrence, prepared to stay. "Lord Brynne, good afternoon," he began politely, moving towards them with a smile of saintly patience stretching his thin lips. "And Lady Brynne... Charmed and pleased to see you at the Abbey again." Spying Sir Timothy hovering in the background, the vicar winced, then deigned to notice him with a brief nod.

Vicar Beakman was a tall, rather stout man with black hair, quite thin on the top, the sparse strands of which were combed over his shining crown with meticulous care. His nose was curved like an eagle's and of such generous proportions as to make him the ideal recipient of his unfortunate name. He was dressed all in black, the only exception being his neckcloth, which was grey.

"Vicar Beakman, how nice to see you," Lord Brynne lied engagingly. "Allow me to introduce Lord Amesbury and his daughter, Miss Angela Fairfax."

The vicar bowed over her hand, staring at her quite hard and long. The parson in Finchingfield had never looked at her in such a bold way! Angela was close to blushing by the time he finally turned away and said his civil "how d'you dos" to the sleepy Lord Amesbury.

"Is that Miss Beakman I spy behind you, Vicar?" said Lord Brynne when the vicar continued to ignore the young woman with him. "Back from Portsmouth, I see."

Vicar Beakman did not seem very desirous of including his daughter in the group, but Lord Brynne's pointed remark could not be disregarded. Indeed, thought Angela with some astonishment, did he think Miss Beakman could be ignored throughout the entire visit?

"Yes, my Good Samaritan has returned," said the vicar at last with a strained smile. "Come, Charity. Come and meet Lord Brynne's houseguests." Then, scowling in quite a particular way at Sir Timothy, he drew Charity near.

Miss Charity Beakman was nothing like her father. She was a small girl, pale and large-eyed. Her hair, like her eyes, was sherry brown and she would have been exceptionally pretty if only she had smiled and exhibited a little animation. As it was, she stood in the shadow of her large father and stared at the floor. Angela noticed shades of emotions flitting across her small, heart-shaped face. The girl inspired compassion in Angela and she determined then and there to try to make her feel more comfortable.

"You've been away, Miss Beakman?" enquired Angela, smiling encouragingly at the girl. "And on an errand of mercy, I gather?"

"Just last night she returned to me from the home of her Aunt Ruth, my late wife's sister, in Portsmouth," the vicar answered for his daughter. "Ruth was not in ill health when Charity first went to her. Charity only intended to bear the elderly woman company for a time. But Ruth became ill suddenly and did not improve. Charity, in the true Christian spirit, tended her till her death. Since the woman had no children and few friends, Charity stayed on to make sure she was given a proper burial. Her means were extremely modest, if you understand me," he explained with a significant nod. "Charity did not even write to me of her aunt's death, but took care of everything on her own, knowing I had my duties here to think of and not wishing to trouble me. Quite the brave little pilgrim, isn't she? She travelled home in the company of her aunt's servant, who changed coaches in Keswick. Charity had only to travel from there to Rosethwaite alone."

"Goodness, you *are* a brave girl!" opined the dowager, staring at Miss Beakman with open astonishment. "I should have been frightened to death to travel all that way without my papa, or some other male relative, to protect me."

"I did not mind it very much," said Miss Beakman in a shy voice, and looking as though she wished the conversation were not centred round her.

"I'm very sorry to hear of your aunt's death, Miss Beakman," the marquess said kindly. "You must have been attached to her."

"Thank you, my lord," said Miss Beakman, lowering her lashes and returning her gaze to the floor.

"It was her time, my Lord Brynne," the vicar stated dismissively. "We all have our time, and must flee this mortal life to meet our Maker and give an accounting of our earthly deeds. All our actions must be accounted for, whether good—" here he threw a glance towards Sir Timothy "—or bad."

Timothy flushed alarmingly, and Angela began to worry lest a man of the cloth be throttled in the Abbey entry hall. What was amiss between those two? Thankfully the marquess intervened. "Isn't it a blessing that our deeds will be judged by One who has no earthly prejudices to interfere with His justice and mercy?" he said amiably.

Angela felt a little thrill of admiration at the marquess's tactful handling of the situation. In a perfectly civilized manner, and with a smile on his lips, he'd hinted to the vicar that his expressions were less than truly Christian. Now it was the vicar's turn to flush.

Obviously Vicar Beakman disapproved of Sir Timothy. But what had Tim done to earn such apparent scorn?

Setting aside these thoughts to ponder at a later time, Angela spoke to Miss Beakman. "My best bosom-bow in Finchingfield is the daughter of a clergyman, Miss Beakman. I daresay you and I have a great deal in common."

Miss Beakman looked as though she wished it were true and favoured Angela with an uncertain smile.

"Miss Fairfax seems just the sort of girl who would take pleasure in the company of a parson's daughter," said Vicar Beakman approvingly. "Such a sweet-looking young woman," he added, smiling at her in that odious way again. It made her feel like an especially juicy apple tart. Then he cleared his throat and continued, "We have been making social calls, Lord Brynne, and bringing Charity round to see you after an absence of nearly eight months is part of the reason I've come today, but I do have other business I wish to discuss with you."

Pleasantries at an end, everyone went into the drawing-room. The vicar was evidently surprised to discover that he had to conduct his business with Lord Brynne under the curious gaze of several other persons. Angela was not sure of the others' motives for being present, but she had no intention of absenting herself from a conversation which might have something to do with Harry.

Everyone was seated now and the vicar spoke. "Well, my lord, this abandoned child left on the Abbey steps last night...what do you propose to do? You are aware, of course, that it ought to be given to me. I would do what I could for it."

" 'It' is a boy," Angela was quick to inform the vicar. "And his name is Harry." She was dismayed by the vicar's cold manner about something as precious as a small, human life. However, the vicar begged her pardon and acknowledged her point with a gracious nod.

"Surely you've heard through village gossip that I've taken it upon myself to try to find the child's mother," Lord Brynne put in. "Judging by the note his mother left in Harry's basket, she wants me to raise and care for the child. If I were to decide on some other course, I would wish to consult his mother first. Perhaps she can be assisted in some way so that she can keep Harry."

"You do realize that the child is very probably illegitimate?" queried the vicar.

The marquess nodded. "The mother was honest enough to say so."

"In such cases, we generally place the unfortunate child in a foundling home, such as the one I oversee in Keswick. Certainly it was foolish and ill considered of the mother to believe that such a child would be welcome at the Abbey, my lord!"

Lord Brynne raised a brow. "The child cannot help how he came into the world. And I do not think it ill considered of the mother to expect any feeling man to do all he can for Harry."

Once again the vicar was brought to the blush. "Indeed, of course, that is…" he faltered. "You know I did not mean that the child is not worthy of your concern; it's simply that—"

"Do not trouble to explain," the marquess coolly interrupted. "Ordinarily I would not wish to interfere in matters which the church considers within its jurisdiction, but I insist upon interfering in this particular case. I've sent Mr. Holmes about the estate to make enquiries, and I have not lost hope yet that the child's mother may be found. Of course I shall keep you informed." He stood up, clearly indicating that their interview was at an end.

Vicar Beakman also stood up. He looked slightly abashed, as if he knew he had overstepped his bounds and was sorry for it. Striving to mend his fences, he assumed a humble air, smiling and saying, "Thank you, my Lord Brynne. Indeed, I had no wish to meddle. I only thought perhaps I could help in my small way. Do let me know if I can be useful."

By now, Angela had come to the same conclusion about the vicar as had Lord Brynne and Sir Timothy. She could not like him. There was a smug self-righteousness about the man which was quite offensive. He seemed to have too little tolerance and sympathy for those less inclined than himself to be "good." And, lastly, she did not like the way he looked at her, even though she suspected he admired her.

He then bade them all good-afternoon and, with Charity in tow, exited the room. Sir Timothy and Lord Amesbury, though the latter was a trifle unsteady on his feet, bowed them out, while Lord Brynne accompanied them to the door. As soon as the guests had passed through to the hall, Lord Amesbury collapsed on the sofa and went promptly back to sleep.

"The pompous windbag!" exploded Sir Timothy as the closing thud of the Abbey's front door echoed down the hall. "Hardly gave the girl a chance to say 'boo!' I know she's quite capable of speaking for herself. And she's got such a sweet voice, too!"

"Calm down, Tim" advised the marquess, re-entering the room. "You can't blame the vicar for being rather protective of her, you know. He obviously did not know you were here, or else I'm sure he wouldn't have brought her at all!"

"Why does the vicar mistrust Sir Timothy?" asked Angela, her curiosity considerably piqued.

"Must you talk so freely in front of Miss Fairfax?" hissed Lady Brynne, wagging her finger at her son. "Indeed, you forget yourselves!"

Lord Brynne looked meditative, as though he were considering his mother's words. How serious he was, Angela could not say, because a small smile played at the corners of his mouth even while his brows drew together in thought.

"Miss Fairfax has already said that she is well aware of my rakish reputation," his lordship said at last, the small smile quirked into an impish grin as he looked at Angela. "Since I have observed her wit to be unusually sharp in one so young and beautiful, it would not be difficult for her to reason out that Tim is burdened with a similar reputation."

"But the vicar seems particularly to dislike Sir Timothy—" began Angela, not to be diverted by the marquess's dubious compliment.

"Come, my dear," said the dowager, rising decisively and pulling Angela to her feet. "We must get our beauty sleep before dressing for dinner. And, Sydney, wake up Lord Amesbury, if you please," she called over her shoulder, "and send him to bed. He'll develop one of his dreadful cramps if he sleeps too long in that tight corset!"

And thus Angela was borne away to her bedchamber, her mind reeling with unanswered questions. After her abigail undressed her, she slid between the cool sheets of the bed and gave full reign to her churning thoughts. Eventually she dozed. Passing through her dreams was an abandoned babe, a sharp-faced vicar with a doe-eyed daughter—who, by the by, had arrived in Rosethwaite on the same day as Harry—a snoring Papa in a tight corset, a matchmaking dowager, a debauched young man with a penchant for sweet voices, mysterious notes and runaway villains, and a nobleman with teasing blue eyes.... And in her dreams she couldn't quite remember.... Rakes *were* supposed to make bad husbands, weren't they?

CHAPTER FOUR

THAT AFTERNOON a rather sober group gathered round Sydney's dining-table. He reasoned that they were each immersed in thoughts as deep as his own, but that they were centred on the same unwelcome idea was doubtful.

In truth, the vicar's visit, and certain facts revealed during it, had led Sydney down a path of speculation the others would probably never consider, and which, he must admit, he was almost ashamed of. For suddenly Miss Beakman was a suspect in his search for Harry's mother.

That her return to the neighbourhood had coincided with Harry's appearance at the Abbey was not the only reason for his suspicions. But only further observation and enquiry would prove or disprove his developing theory. And, he stressed to himself, it was merely a theory. The chance of his being wrong was as great as the chance of his being right. In the meantime, since the mystery could not possibly be solved that evening, he meant to prod his guests out of their collective brown study and amuse himself.

After dinner, Sydney rushed Lord Amesbury through his port and Tim through his cheroots so that they entered the drawing-room fast on the heels of his mother and Miss Fairfax. That young lady had looked especially fetching at dinner in a pale blue satin underdress, covered with delicate netting and trimmed at the bodice and short, puffed sleeves with cockle-shells and satin. She had been preoccupied for the most part, that tiny fissure of worry between her brows appearing from time to time throughout the meal.

Obviously, Miss Fairfax was taking Harry's plight much to heart. An unexpected prick of domestic feeling stirred in Sydney's chest at the idea of her worrying over the child, just as Caroline used to worry over Wellesley when he had a chill or some other childhood illness. He must have been missing Wellesley to have been so unaccountably reminded of Caroline, he decided.

When they entered the drawing-room, his mother had already ordered tea and Miss Fairfax was pouring it out. After reacquainting herself with how the gentlemen preferred their tea, Miss Fairfax helped them each to a cup. Another surge of homely feeling flowed through him at the sight of the young lady's graceful handling of the teapot, her slim, elegant hands holding and caressing the china as if she relished the feel of it. And it was altogether charming the way one plump yellow ringlet fell over her white bosom as she bent to procure her father a spoonful of sugar.

Well, perhaps the vision of the round, dancing ringlet against her pale skin was not wholly spurred by domestic inclination, he admitted to himself as his pulse skittered like a frisky colt. Nor could he truly convince himself that he merely admired Miss Fairfax's efficiency as hostess at the teapot; in fact, he was much more intrigued with the play of her fingers against the china. Perhaps Tim was right, and beneath her disarmingly angelic façade she was a passionate creature. Sensuous was a more apt term, he decided, as he continued to watch her.

Reaching for a stem of grapes, Tim leaned near and whispered, "You look like a starved urchin at the bakery window, Syd!" Sydney gave his friend an irritated frown, but the pithy comment served to remind him of his policy concerning innocents. He firmly repeated to himself the list of reasons why green girls were a hazard to a rake's well-being, strived to calm himself and sat down. Upon consideration, he was appalled to have discovered that his body quickened by the mere sight of a chit pouring tea. As to why he sat directly across from the sweet confection called Angela Fairfax, and with just such a view as would put a strain on his resolve, he did not dare to consider.

Clearing his throat and determined to put a damper on his rising desire, he said, "Have you seen Harry this afternoon, Miss Fairfax?" He languidly stirred his own cup of brew, which, as was his custom, he balanced on his knee. Miss Fairfax had done with helping the others and he watched her lift a delicate bone-china cup to her lips.

"Why, yes I have," she answered promptly and brightly, the cup poised at a point exactly level with her breasts. A tendril of steam twined lazily through the air towards her chin. It rather vaguely occurred to Sydney that the tea must be hot.

"And he is doing well, I take it?" Sydney prompted her, anxious to encourage some diverting conversation.

Miss Fairfax's brows drew together and she pursed her rosebud lips. Sydney's eyes were drawn to those lips. Puckered just so they looked wickedly kissable. "Well, my lord, he is not exactly in 'prime twig' at the moment, as Fran put it. I daresay he is teething or some such thing. Fran says he's drooling like the sap runs in the spring."

Sydney laughed, the china cup rattling on its dish, the tea lapping against the rim. "Fran seems to have a plethora of colourful expressions!"

"Watch your cup, Sydney, the tea is too hot," advised his mother. "Fran is doing an excellent job, isn't she? The housekeeper says Harry has quite attached himself to Fran," she further informed Lord Amesbury, who sat at her elbow in a wing-chair.

"I'm devilish glad to hear it, my dear, er, Lady Brynne," responded Lord Amesbury with a drowsy smile for the dowager.

"Don't know if it's such a good thing, really," observed Tim, who stood by the fireplace now, his legs crossed at the ankle, one elbow resting on the low Adam mantelpiece.

"What do you mean, Tim?" asked the dowager, startled.

"He probably means that since Harry isn't going to be staying here, he ought not to get too attached to anyone," explained Sydney. Miss Fairfax still held her cup several inches from her lips and Sydney waited expectantly for her finally to take a sip. He was mortified by his eagerness, deeming it foolishness beyond anything to be lusting after a woman who sat in broad daylight, fully clothed, in the company of her father and his mother, and who was merely drinking tea.

"Since we are going to find Harry's mother, I daresay he will forget Fran soon enough," Miss Fairfax opined. "Nothing is like a mother's love, after all." Finally Miss Fairfax lifted her cup. Her lips parted . . .

"Miss Fairfax, stop a moment!" the dowager exclaimed, touching her arm lightly. "The tea is quite scalding! I shall have to speak to Lawrence about it. I daresay we have a new maid in the kitchen. Better cool it with a little cream, my dear."

Miss Fairfax blinked once or twice, lowered the cup, observed the steaming liquid and said, "Why, yes, it is rather hot, isn't it? My mind has been a thousand miles away this afternoon. Ever since the vicar... That is, ever since we went to the George today!"

Sydney cursed himself for a fool. He should have warned her about the tea, but he had only vaguely registered the fact that it was hot himself. Then he slavishly watched as she laced her tea with a generous dollop of cool cream and began to stir it.

Finally she lifted the cup and took a swallow. Her lips lingered on the smooth, warm rim of the cup longer than necessary and when she set it down on the dish, her thumb stroked the delicate handle in an absent-minded caress. Miss Fairfax had a way of drinking tea, he decided, swallowing nervously. He wasn't sure why he'd never noticed before, but it was obvious, by the way she handled the china, that she had a sensuous soul.

The thought was not a soothing one. Grimly determined to ignore Miss Fairfax's blatant, though quite unconscious, sensuality, he lifted his own cup of tea for a fortifying drink.

"Good God!" he exclaimed as the scalding liquid seared his lips. The cup was returned with a loud chink to the dish and placed speedily on the table by his chair. He snatched a serviette and pressed it against his burning lips.

"Sydney, did you not hear me say just now that the tea was scalding?" admonished his mother. "Are you burnt, my dear?"

Everyone was watching him, albeit with alarm and concern in their expressions, but it was deuced embarrassing. And Tim—blast the cur!—looked almost triumphant.

"Cold water ought to do the trick, my lord," offered Miss Fairfax, her soft grey eyes sympathetic. Little did the chit know that *she* was the cause of his inattention to such minor details as scalding liquid! "My lady, perhaps you ought to send the footman for some very cold water," she repeated to the dowager. "If Lord Brynne will dip his handkerchief in the water and place it on his lips, it will take the heat out and keep the burn from blistering."

The dowager followed Miss Fairfax's advice and a footman was dispatched to do her bidding. Mean-

while, Sydney sat in mortified silence, his chin resting
in his hand and his long fingers curved round his
throbbing mouth.

"How did you know what to do, Miss Fairfax?"
asked Tim, no doubt impressed by her practical
knowledge.

"I daresay she read it somewhere," Sydney mumbled from behind his hand.

"Quite right, my lord," she admitted, not the least
ashamed to own to a little bookishness. "Does it hurt
to talk?"

"Not enough to silence me, I'm afraid," he said
wryly.

"Oh, I should not wish for *that*," she assured him,
her eyes twinkling. "Sometimes I find your conversation quite diverting!"

"Only *sometimes?*" he quizzed her.

"Well, a diversion from the task which has lately
kept us occupied is exactly what we need tonight,"
Tim stated firmly. "It's my opinion that we've spent
time and thought enough for one day on that little
ragamuffin upstairs. 'Tis a sobering subject and it is
turning us all into dull dogs indeed! There's nothing
else to be done tonight, so why don't we play cards, or
sing duets, or... or... something!"

By now the footman had returned with the water
and Sydney had dipped his handkerchief in the bowl
and was pressing the healing cold water against his
lips. He was already feeling much better.

"Well, if none of you mind, I'm going to lie down
on that yonder couch and take a little nap," Lord

Amesbury presently announced, stretching and yawning like a great bear.

"Goodness, Papa!" exclaimed Miss Fairfax. "As much as you nap during the day, one would almost think you do not sleep a wink at night!"

Sydney observed the deeper rose showing through his mother's rouged cheeks and Lord Amesbury's guilty sidelong glance in her direction. So his mama's relationship with Lord Amesbury was as friendly as that, was it? He had suspected as much by the way she looked at the portly old gent, and bits of warm conversation he'd chanced to hear by accident. She must be in love! Well, he was in favour of anything, or anybody, that made her happy, though Lord Amesbury was certainly nothing like his father!

"Some of us have difficulty sleeping at night, Miss Fairfax," Sydney spoke up, gallantly coming to his blushing mother's rescue. "For one reason or another."

"Yes!" Tim agreed, his expression lighting up suddenly. "For example, there's Spindle-shanks and Willy. They've been known to disturb a person's sleep now and then!"

"Goodness, who are you speaking of, Sir Timothy? Spindle-shanks seems a very odd name!" said Miss Fairfax.

"An odd name for an odd fellow, Miss Fairfax," returned Tim, his eyes twinkling with mischief. "Would you like me to tell you about him?"

Sydney groaned. "Now you have done it, Miss Fairfax. Tim's itching for some diversion, and he positively loves to tell ghost stories! And if you encourage him by shivering and turning pale, you must be prepared to listen to his ghastly tales all night!''

"Ghosts! You have ghosts at the Abbey?'' Miss Fairfax clapped her hands in delight. "How capital!''

"Dear, you mustn't take Tim and Sydney too seriously, you know,'' advised the dowager, frowning at the two gentlemen. "I, for one, have never seen a ghost at the Abbey, and I doubt very much that one exists. Do not be frightened by these careless fellows' teasing.''

"Oh, but I'm not frightened,'' she assured the dowager. "Do tell me about Spindle-shanks, Sir Timothy!''

"Wait a minute,'' said Sydney, dropping the serviette on the tray by the bowl. "Are you telling me, Miss Fairfax, that the idea of ghosts haunting the Abbey does not disturb you?''

"Indeed, my lord, I was hoping the Abbey had a ghost. In my opinion, no ancient building is worth its salt unless it has a spectre or two to haunt its halls!''

Sydney was astonished. He observed her silently for a moment, then leaned forward a little and in a half whisper, said, "The idea of a restless spirit with head in hand making you a midnight call, or a sin-burdened, mournful apparition dragging his heavy chains past your bedchamber door in the wee, dark hours of the morning does not inspire you to reach for your vinaigrette, Miss Fairfax?''

"If I thought you had spirits of such a deplorable description, my lord, of course I'd be frightened. But

surely nothing so sinister could haunt such a delightful place as the Abbey. I'm persuaded your ghosts are
perfectly harmless.''

Sydney was charmed by Miss Fairfax's explanation
for her relative calm in the face of supernatural possibilities. Despite the fact that it hurt his injured lips
to do so, he couldn't help but smile. ''You're quite
correct, Miss Fairfax. The personalities of Castlerigg's resident ghosts run much more to the benign
than the tortured. In fact, our two most famous spirits, Spindle-shanks and Willy, are rather comical.''

Vastly enjoying himself, Sydney was about to
launch into an explanation when he remembered Tim.
''Oh dear, I'd quite forgotten that you meant to tell
the story, Tim. Pray excuse me and carry on!''

Tim had removed to a chair by the fire and looked
perfectly comfortable. ''No, Syd,'' he said with a lazy
smile. ''Really, you go ahead. They're your ghosts,
after all!''

''Well, I do hope you'll excuse me, Lord Brynne,''
said Lord Amesbury, standing and bowing at the waist
till his corset creaked. ''While I find the subject altogether—'' he stopped and yawned hugely ''—fascinating, I couldn't keep my eyes open for the King
himself!''

''Indeed, Lord Amesbury, go to sleep if you must,''
admonished Sydney cheerfully. ''One has to get one's
rest sometime, doesn't one?''

Lord Amesbury gave him a look that was both
puzzled and alarmed, but Sydney smiled back so in-

genuously that his lordship was satisfied and lumbered off to his couch without further ado.

"Dear fellow," clucked the dowager. "I do hope sleeping in that corset won't give him the cramp!"

"Well, if it does, perhaps he'll quit wearing the silly thing," said Angela practically. "Now, Lord Brynne, if you don't tell me about your ghosts I shall scream! Begin with Spindle-shanks, if you please!"

Miss Fairfax sat forward in her chair, her eyes sparkling like diamonds, her small hands clasped together tightly. Sydney could not resist such an eager, not to mention delectable, audience. He gave a courtly little nod of his head and said, "I'm at your command, Miss Fairfax. But first let me tell you a little history of the Abbey. It was erected just prior to King Henry the Eighth's edict in 1539 to suppress all monastic orders in England. The Abbey and its surrounding farmlands were given to a nobleman favoured by the King and soon thereafter purchased by an ancestor of mine. He promptly died and left the Abbey to his only heir, our own Spindle-shanks. His real name was Fenius Bartholomew St. James, my great-great-great uncle, I believe. He was a foppish fellow, Miss Fairfax, whose skinny legs did not show to advantage in the leggings which were so fashionable in his time, which is how he got pegged 'Spindle-shanks,' or 'Skinny-legs,' as it is said in the more proper vernacular."

"Oh, I see!" said Miss Fairfax with a fervid little flutter of her hands which was quite flattering to Sydney's skill as a story-teller. "Do go on!"

"Well, it seems that Fenius was never particularly enamoured of the Abbey, but since it was his sole inheritance and its estate the means of his comfortable income, he was obliged to visit it from time to time. Otherwise he would have been perfectly content to beguile away his days at Court in London. He lived for Society and suffered greatly when he was compelled to rusticate in Cumberland on some business or other. On one such obligatory trip to the Abbey, he was expecting a visit from the King. Delirious with joy and proud anticipation, he wore himself down till he caught a violent cold. He died the very day King Henry was expected!"

"Oh, dear, how dreadful for him to have missed such a visitor!" said Miss Fairfax.

"Indeed!" agreed Sydney soberly. "Denied such a prestigious event, he's never rested peacefully since, but walks the galleries on occasion and has been frequently seen bowing before the portrait of King Henry in the main hall!"

"Poppycock," observed Lady Brynne, quite calmly nibbling on a brandy-snap. "*I've* never seen him!"

"Disbelievers never do," Sydney replied irrepressibly.

"Oh, I do hope *I* see him!" said Miss Fairfax. "But now what of this Willy fellow?"

"Pray, Sydney, do not tell her about Willy," objected the dowager fretfully. "The less airing of our dirty linen the better!"

"But Willy's the best of all!" said Tim from his distant chair. "If you don't tell her about Willy, I shall be forced to tell her some of my own grim tales of Windy Grange!''

"You must concede, Mama, that *that* will never do," said Sydney, favouring his mother with an apologetic smile. "Willy it is."

Lady Brynne *hmmphed* disdainfully.

"Was he another of your relatives, my lord?" prompted Miss Fairfax.

"No, Willy was a stable-boy. But he had conceived an infatuation for my grandmother, Harriet. Grandfather took objection to the moonling's devotion, however, when the lad began sneaking into the house at odd hours to press his suit! Grandfather chased Willy through the Abbey one night after he found him crouched in grandmother's wardrobe. The poor fellow stumbled on the stairs and broke his neck!"

"How shocking!"

"Yes, but it did have its compensations. Grandmother seemed convinced of her husband's love after that episode. It had been in question before, you understand, since he was a flirtatious fellow. They got along famously from then on. And when a handkerchief full of Grandmother's jewels was found in the deceased Willy's pocket, they realized he would have been hanged for his crimes anyway, relieving Grandfather of some of his regret over the incident. But now Willy seems determined to vex all progeny of the late Claudius St. James by playing irritating, but harmless, pranks on them. If ever you lose something, Miss Fairfax, or discover something rearranged, you must consider the possibility that Willy has been afoot!"

"How fascinating, my lord!"

"And how utterly ridiculous," added the dowager. "I've never lost anything at the Abbey which hasn't been accounted for in some logical way. Make no doubt, Miss Fairfax, someone, probably my father, concocted these ghost stories one cold night in February when he had little better to do!"

"Perhaps Miss Fairfax prefers to believe otherwise, Mama," said Sydney, admiring the young lady's animated countenance.

"I own I do rather like to believe in the wonderful, the magical, the mysterious! It makes life much more of an adventure, I think."

"Ah, but wonders and magic are so hard to come by in these modern days," observed the marquess, unable to restrain the rather pensive note in his voice.

"Mysteries are plentiful enough," said the dowager repressively. "And we've got quite enough mysteries on our hands with little Harry to worry about. We certainly needn't dredge up the Abbey ghosts! Nor do I wish to hear about Tim's bugbears at the Grange, either! I had much rather have a game or two of Macao or Picquet!"

Sydney could see that his mother's patience was at its limit. Evidently, Miss Fairfax and Tim saw it, too, and went with polite docility to the card-table. Despite the young people being denied a more lively occupation, the evening passed pleasantly. Lord Amesbury's snoring remained at a tolerable level, and the fire crackled merrily in the grate.

At least the others seemed comfortable and happy enough, thought Sydney rather ruefully. His peace, however, was quite cut up by a return of his earlier lustful thoughts concerning Miss Fairfax. Sitting just next to her, Sydney was beguiled by the light lavender scent which seemed to surround her. And must she brush the cards against her bottom lip just so? It was deuced distracting! And had she ought, when thinking how to play her next turn, to twirl her fingers through that blasted golden ringlet which shone so lustrously in the candlelight? A bad habit, that!

"Sydney, you're playing like a flat," Tim stated grimly. "Good thing we're not up against a couple of sharps, or we'd be cleaned out of all our ready of a certainty. Your mother and Miss Fairfax have us about dished up as it is!"

Sydney apologized and scowled determinedly at his cards. "Whose turn is it, anyway?" he grumbled.

THAT NIGHT Angela prepared for bed with a head bursting with new impressions and ideas. It had been quite an eventful day, certainly a much more exciting day than she was used to having at Amesbury Manor in Finchingfield.

She'd looked in on Harry, who'd been put in the nursery and was comfortably ensconced there with Fran, and, of course, Zeus, who reclined on the hearthrug. Harry had been made quite a fuss of in the kitchen, Fran said, and she'd put him to bed with a full stomach and a dry napkin, tucked all round with a flannel blanket. Harry smiled in his sleep and An-

gela felt she could rest easy about him, at least for the
night.

Besides, foremost in her thoughts was the marquess. Angela snuggled between the bedclothes and
stretched her cold feet towards the warmth emanating
from the hot brick the chambermaid had tucked at the
foot of her bed. The fire burnt briskly still in the bedchamber's fireplace, and she did not wish to draw her
bedcurtains. The fact was, she decided, as she lay there
in the partial darkness, she *liked* the marquess!

For one thing, he was extremely entertaining! He
always had interesting things to say and seemed quite
well-informed on any number of subjects. From some
of their conversations, she'd discovered that he took
an active part in the House of Lords. She hadn't expected such industry from a rake. And he was very
kind, too. He treated his servants exceptionally well
and seemed genuinely concerned over Harry's fate and
was going to a great deal of trouble to find the babe's
mother. She liked the way he had stood up to the vicar,
and with such tact, too! All in all, she had to admit
that he was proving to be quite wonderful in every respect—except one.

Angela frowned. Why must he be a rake? Perhaps
it ran in the family—hadn't he said that his grandmother had doubted his grandfather's love because he
was "flirtatious"? Was that Lord Brynne's diplo-
matic way of saying that his grandfather had by-blows
scattered about the countryside? It was too puzzling,
and much too tiring a question to tackle so late at
night. Angela drifted off to sleep.

It might have been a minute later, or an hour, or perhaps half the night, but Angela was awake after a singularly unrestful period of slumber. The room was nearly black, the embers of her fire barely glowing. What had woken her?

She sat up in bed and peered about her in the dark, looking for she knew not what. Suddenly she heard a noise coming from somewhere outside her door, like shuffling and thudding, and . . . muffled cursing! The first hopeful thought that came to her mind was that one of the Abbey ghosts was being uncommonly clumsy tonight and had perhaps stubbed his supernatural toe against a jutting floorboard! It was an absurd idea and made her giggle, but she was determined to investigate.

Then a much more sobering thought came to her. What if the noise was coming from a completely human, very much alive person with mischief on his mind? Harry's father, perhaps. But since the nursery was situated on the upper floor, at least Harry was in no immediate danger. Besides, Lord Brynne kept a secure house and it seemed quite unlikely that someone could get in without rousing the servants. Perhaps what she was hearing *was* a servant.

She reached for the candle and tinder-box on her bedside table, struck a light and lit the taper. Extending her candle in front of her, she slipped out of bed and opened the door leading into the gallery. Flipping her long braid of golden hair over her shoulder, she stepped into the dark corridor, which was lit by a single lamp at the very end. She looked first to the right and then to the left. . . . What was that? It was like the tail-end of a nightdress wisping round the corner towards the other wing.

Practically strangled by her own nervous excitement, she quickly stepped forward and reached the corner round which the person, or thing, had vanished. Turning the corner, she held her candle out and looked very hard into the murky darkness of the adjacent hall. Then she saw it. It was . . . Good God, it was her father! What was he doing up at this hour, and where was he going?

Then it struck her. That was the marchioness's door he was creeping towards! Though Angela hardly knew her way round the large Abbey yet, she was familiar with the location of the dowager's bedchamber, because she had been summoned there once and guided by a servant. Try as she might, Angela could conceive of only one reason for her father to be visiting their hostess at this late hour. Her father and the Marchioness of Brynne were *lovers!*

Perhaps her father had heard her gasp of astonishment, because he was turning round. Goodness, he mustn't see her! How mortifying for both of them if he did!

Quickly Angela snuffed her candle, burning her fingers in the process, and backed into the closest recess in the wall, which happened to be the door to yet another chamber. She pressed herself snugly against the smooth wood and held her breath. Straining to hear whether her father was coming towards her, or whether he were indeed entering the marchioness's

bedchamber, she stood perfectly still. Soon, the slight
click of the door opening and shutting and a muffled
murmur of welcome reached her. Heaving a sigh of
relief, Angela was suddenly aware of her burning fingers and popped them in her mouth.

"Goodness," she muttered round her fingers,
"what else can happen!"

It seemed that very much more could indeed happen, and the first thing was that the door she was
leaning against opened. Down she toppled like a felled
oak, but she did not hit the floor. Strong arms grasped
her about the waist and her head thumped against
something which managed to be both soft and hard.
It was a man's chest. In fact, it was Lord Brynne's
chest.

"Miss Fairfax," he murmured, astonishment evi-
dent in his deep voice. "I thought I heard something!
What are you doing in my doorway?"

Angela scampered to her feet and turned to face
him. Speech was not immediately within her power.
Lord Brynne, seeming to understand that she was
somewhat at a loss, pushed her into a nearby chair and
quietly closed the door.

While her faculties were not especially sharp, it did
occur to Angela that it was not precisely wise, or
seemly, to be shut up in his lordship's bedchamber.
She started to stand up. "M-my lord, I mustn't st-
stay.... I mean, this is your bedchamber, is...is it not?
And why, pray, d-did you shut the door?"

Lord Brynne placed his hands gently on her shoulders and sat her down again. "Do you want to wake

up the house, Miss Fairfax, and let them find you in my bedchamber?''

"I did not mean to c-come here, my lord, I was j-just..." Angela's voice trailed off.

"Stalking spirits?"

"Well, I h-heard sounds in the hall outside my door and I thought..."

"Hush a moment, child," Lord Brynne soothed. "Before you say another word, we had better strive to restore a little colour to your cheeks. I've a remedy that will help that stutter, too! You have need of a fortifying drink of Scotch whisky!"

Then, after ascertaining that Angela had no intention of sliding out of the chair and onto the floor, Lord Brynne walked to a nearby table, picked up a crystal decanter and poured a small amount of amber liquid into a glass. He snatched a look at her, and evidently perceiving that she might be in need of more than the usual restorative dose, doubled the amount.

"Can you hold it, or shall I help you?"

"I c-can certainly hold it myself!" retorted Angela with as much dignity as she could muster. Then, after three or four generous sips of the stuff, Angela coughed, felt the blood return to her head in a throbbing rush, and handed the almost empty glass to the marquess.

Lord Brynne had knelt on the floor to hand Angela the whisky, and now sat back on his heels to observe her. "Now, Miss Fairfax," he said, "perhaps you can tell me what sort of an adventure you've been up to!"

Angela lifted her eyes and saw the marquess as if for the first time since she'd entered, or rather plummeted into, the room. It was not his bedchamber, but rather a sort of antechamber, or an attached private parlour, with a desk and bookshelves and comfortable furniture scattered about. All this she could see by the light of a brisk fire burning on the grate. There were no candles, just the firelight, and everything glowed soft and rosy. Even the marquess . . .

"Good heavens, my lord," she burst out. "You're in your nightshirt!"

"And, you, Miss Fairfax, are in your nightdress!" he promptly returned.

"And you're wearing a nightcap, too," she continued, fascination with her discovery overriding her embarrassment. "I had not thought that rakes wore nightcaps!"

"Well, I can assure you, on the best authority, that rakes feel the cold, too. Especially," he emphasized with a wicked gleam in his eyes, "when they sleep alone."

This comment served to remind Angela of where she was, and with whom she was having this odd conversation. "I beg your pardon, my lord, I did not think . . ."

"You did not think rakes wore anything to bed, I suppose," he finished for her.

"I never meant to say anything of the sort, sir," Angela retorted, standing up abruptly and swaying a little as the whisky, no doubt, sloshed about in her head. "And now I mean to return to my room!"

"Not before you tell me why you were leaning against my bedchamber door, Miss Fairfax," he informed her in an uncompromising tone of voice, standing up and towering over her. "Did you think, perhaps, you saw a ghost?"

"Would rather have seen a ghost than what I saw" was her sulky reply.

"Oh, I see," said Lord Brynne, a knowing look coming over his face. "You saw your papa, er, visiting my mother's room."

"You knew?" she demanded. "Who else knows, pray tell?"

"I haven't the slightest idea, nor do I care. They are quite grown up now and must make their own decisions. Do you disapprove of my mother, Miss Fairfax?"

"No, not at all, my lord. It's just that I didn't expect them to...well...share a bedchamber until they married."

"Perhaps they shan't marry at all," suggested the marquess, with an elegant shrug.

"Not marry?" said Angela scornfully. "Then I certainly don't understand why they're...well... indulging in such behaviour!"

Lord Brynne chuckled deep in his throat. "What an enigma you are, Miss Fairfax. You tolerate me and Tim, fully aware of our lurid reputations, and even go so far as to grant us good traits despite our rakish ways. Yet you do not extend the same generosity to your own father."

"Well, that's just it. He *is* my father, Lord Brynne. I do not expect such behaviour from *him!*"

"He's only human, Miss Fairfax," the marquess gently reminded her. "As are we all."

"But how do you feel about your mother's conduct?"

"I'm delighted to know she is enjoying your father's, er, attentions. Widowhood can be lonely. She's human, too."

Looking up into Lord Brynne's teasing blue eyes, Angela herself felt altogether too human. She was startled to discover his nearness was more dizzying than the effects of the whisky he'd given her. From the nightcap set at a rakish angle on his tousled dark hair, to the slight stubble of beard on his chin, the sensuous curve of his mouth, the wide shoulders encased in soft muslin, narrowing to slim hips and muscular legs protruding from the bottom of his nightshirt, Lord Brynne oozed masculinity.

Angela's eyes were drawn back to his lips. She remembered how he'd burnt them earlier on scalding tea and an empathetic shudder rippled through her. "They didn't blister, I see," she said, lifting a finger and lightly tracing the upper curve of his mouth.

"Good night, Miss Fairfax," the marquess said abruptly and in a very gruff voice.

Startled, Angela drew back her hand and looked into his eyes. They gleamed as brightly as jewels and seemed to hold a warning. "Good night, Lord Brynne," she returned in a small voice, backing away and out the door before she realized she hadn't a candle to see her way to her room.

Lord Brynne appeared at the door and thrust a lighted candle through it. "Mind your step," he advised. And then the door was firmly shut and he was gone.

CHAPTER FIVE

ANGELA WAS GENERALLY an early riser. However, this morning she was loath to leave her bed. Having nearly bumped into her papa in the gallery the night before, and then been privy to the disturbing sight of her rakish host decked out in nightshirt and cap, she felt unequal to facing either of them at the breakfast table. Embarrassed confusion enveloped her as she remembered how she'd touched his lordship's lips. What had possessed her to do such a thing? Indeed, it was as if she had been *compelled* to touch him! Such a strong compulsion was frightening, and perhaps, the nagging voice of her conscience suggested, even a little wicked!

Angela sighed and turned to rest her chin on her hand, staring towards the easterly facing window. The curtains had been drawn back by a chambermaid and bright autumn sunlight dappled the several small panes. It promised to be a fair day, and ordinarily she would have hurried outside for a ramble after breakfast, but today she lay abed like some elegant London lady who'd been dancing till dawn.

Angela would have preferred to think herself lazy, or elegant, or anything other than cowardly, but she knew it was cowardice that kept her from showing her face belowstairs. What would the marquess say to her? How could she bear to look at her papa and Lady Brynne, acting as though she knew nothing of their behaviour? Had she ought to disapprove of them, or was it acceptable for unmarried persons of an advanced age to carouse together? Perhaps even they, in their elderly years, had feelings similar to those she'd felt last night in Lord Brynne's bedchamber? *Human* feelings, the marquess had called them. But were such feelings natural in a maiden like herself, or, as her conscience kept suggesting, were they wicked?

Pondering these weighty questions, Angela watched as a little brown dab of a bird bounced back and forth along the window-ledge, chirping a morning greeting. A cheerful fire warmed the room and a willow green, muslin day dress was laid out on a wing-chair by the bed, awaiting her pleasure. She'd enjoyed a cup of chocolate and a fresh-baked bilberry muffin brought up to her on a tray by a chambermaid. She'd sent word to the others that she meant to break her fast alone, due, so she'd said, to a lingering headache. Now it was eleven o'clock and Angela was bored. She simply had to summon up all her courage and face the day before it was quite over.

"I wonder what sort of a brier thicket I shall fling myself into today?" she muttered to herself as she eased out from beneath her bedclothes and moved to stand by the window. "I daresay there's not the slightest reason to get up, anyway!" Then, as if providence were inspired to intervene after she'd expressed such a gloomy opinion, Angela saw a man on a horse cantering through the lodge gates and up the drive. She recognized Mr. Holmes, Lord Brynne's steward. They'd met briefly yesterday when she had been walking in the gardens with Lady Brynne.

"How selfish I've been!" Angela said to herself, at the sight of Mr. Holmes. "I'd quite forgotten little Harry in all this silly falderal over rakes in nightcaps and passionate papas! Here is Mr. Holmes come to give Lord Brynne his report, which is something of much greater importance, indeed!" She decided that she had best dress immediately and see what information he'd grubbed up about Harry's mother. She reached for the bell-pull to summon her abigail, and trying to hasten that lady's task in putting her to order, she proceeded vigorously to drag a brush through her dishevelled golden locks till her scalp tingled.

Despite her eager assistance to the abigail, dressing took just as long as ever, and it was a full half-hour before Angela hastily strode into the drawing-room, where she discovered her papa alone with Lady Brynne. The dowager was sitting on a sofa near the fire and her papa stood just behind, his grey head bent low over her shoulder.

Since Lady Brynne held a circle of cloth in one hand and a threaded embroidery needle in the other, one would suppose that Lord Amesbury had been admiring her handiwork, but it did not seem probable that the look of soft rapture on her face was the result of joyful needleworking. Perhaps he'd been nibbling her ear!

Whatever they had been doing, they started guiltily when they looked up and perceived her standing just inside the door. Angela fought back the blush she felt creeping up her neck and said, "Good morning, Papa, Lady Brynne." Then before they could collect their thoughts and reply, she hurriedly enquired, "Where are Lord Brynne and Sir Timothy? I thought I saw Mr. Holmes coming up the drive. Is there word about Harry?"

"How is your headache, my dear?" asked the dowager distractedly, as Lord Amesbury straightened himself with a creak and moved round to the front of the sofa. "You quite surprised us just now. I was about to come up and see how you fared. Had you ought to be up? I've a medicinal draught you might want to try—"

"Thank you! My headache is completely gone," said Angela, trying hard to sound natural and at the same time curb her rising impatience. "But I'm excessively curious about Mr. Holmes and what he's discovered about—"

"You look a little flushed, my pet," interrupted her papa, fidgeting with his quizzing glass. "Are you sure you're feeling quite the thing?"

"Papa! Indeed, I feel splendid!" exclaimed Angela, exasperated. "But I do so wish that I might be told what's happened this morning! I saw Mr. Holmes approaching the house not more than thirty minutes ago. Is he still here?"

"Mr. Holmes has come and gone," said Lord Amesbury. "It was a dashed short visit, wasn't it, my lady?"

"Indeed!" agreed the dowager.

"But what did he say?"

"We haven't the slightest idea, my dear," said Lady Brynne, her nerves restored to their usual complacency. "Sydney and Tim are in the library still, and haven't stirred since Mr. Holmes left. We've been a bit curious ourselves, but were hesitant to disturb them. I daresay they shall come out soon and tell us everything," she finished composedly.

"Well, I shan't wait a moment longer," Angela declared, lifting her chin. "In which direction is the library, Lady Brynne?"

"Third door on the left down the main hall, my dear. But why trouble yourself? Sit down and be comfortable. They'll be along presently. Ah, she's gone. Percy, dearest, is your daughter always so dreadfully determined? You never told me that about her!"

Lord Amesbury frowned thoughtfully. "Indeed, my plum, I never noticed it before!"

"No doubt she is concerned about Harry, but such force of will is uncommon in so young a girl. I do hope she does not spoil her chances with Sydney."

Lord Amesbury's indolent eyes widened. "More the like he'll spoil his chances with her if he does not stubble himself!" he retorted indignantly. "Such wild talk, and right in front of my innocent angel! Sometimes I wonder if I did wrong bringing her here,

Maddy. It doesn't seem to me that your son has the slightest intention of reforming!'' He sat down heavily beside her.

"Calm yourself, Percy,'' soothed the dowager, dropping her piece of stitchery to trail her fingers along his lordship's fat thigh. "As I told you, marriage will change Sydney. He was a doting husband to Caroline.''

"But was he faithful?'' demanded Lord Amesbury, uncharacteristically oblivious to the dowager's playful fondling.

Lady Brynne's delicate brows lifted. "And is that important to you, Percy? I daresay faithfulness is not the general rule once a marriage has progressed beyond the honeymoon stage.'' Then, sidling closer, "Do *you* intend to be faithful, my tiger?''

This got Lord Amesbury's attention and he fixed his beloved with an indulgent eye. "How could I be anything but faithful, my dish? My nights are quite taken up, as well you know. And my days are necessarily spent in resting and building up my strength for the nights!'' His thick brows furrowed. "Do you think the others have noticed?''

"What, my love? That you eat and sleep the better part of the day?'' enquired the dowager, fingering the bottom button of his straining waistcoat. "But I do not know how you behaved before I met you, love. Is it unusual for you to spend your time thusly?''

Lord Amesbury's brows dipped again in deep thought. "Well, I daresay I did eat a little less than I do now, and was not so tired. I was used to having only one, or possibly two, naps a day before I met you, Maddy."

"Poor dear," purred the dowager, nuzzling her head beneath his two chins. "I do hope I make your exertions worthwhile!"

Lord Amesbury gathered her small frame against his massive chest as if she were no more than a kitten, gave her rounded bottom a lingering caress and said, "Indeed you do, Maddy. Now, if only we could be married! Treading the galleries in the dead of night is a dashed draughty business."

"That, my love, must depend on our children," said the dowager in a muffled whisper, since her face was buried in his lordship's elaborate neckcloth. "We must wait and hope."

Lord Amesbury's only reply was a long and lusty sigh.

No FOOTMAN stood at the entrance to the library, and after lightly rapping her knuckles against the heavy wood, Angela opened the door and stepped in. Lord Brynne, dressed in a jacket of deep Bishop's blue, had been sitting behind a large desk by the window with Sir Timothy directly across from him, slumped in a chair. They both stood up when she entered.

"Good morning, Miss Fairfax," said the marquess. She felt him watching her as she walked from the door to the desk. She was quite sure she was blushing. He motioned to the chair next to Tim. "Sit down, won't you? I can guess why you're here. You know Mr. Holmes has made his report to me. But are you fully recovered from your, er, indisposition?'' he added politely.

Angela darted him a suspicious glance, found that she could not read his thoughts by the cast of his countenance and crisply replied, ''I am quite well, thank you!'' She sat down and so did the gentlemen. Then she tried to observe the two men from beneath lowered lashes till their sober expressions, especially Tim's began to alarm her. ''Well, what is it?'' she asked them at last, her embarrassment determinedly set aside in her concern for Harry. ''Do you know who the mother is?''

''Possibly we do, Miss Fairfax'' replied the marquess.

''But then again we could be quite wrong!'' interrupted Sir Timothy, his mouth set in a stern line.

''Very true, Tim!'' agreed Lord Brynne.

''Please explain!'' prompted Angela, sitting forward in her chair.

''According to Mr. Holmes,'' said the marquess, standing up again and pacing the floor in front of the fireplace, his hands stuffed into the little pockets at the top of his pantaloons, ''the tenants claimed complete ignorance of any woman in the region having borne a child in the past several months, except for those mothers who've kept their babes, of course.''

''Of course!'' agreed Angela, wishing he'd sit down. Pacing the hearthrug in that way only drew attention to the magnificent line of his legs, disrupting her concentration to an uncomfortable degree!

"Mr. Holmes was about to concede defeat when something happened which gave him pause. He was leaving the O'Malleys' cottage when the matriarch of the family—Granny Meg, they call her—who is said to be *fey,* or with apartments to let, depending on whom you talk to, detained him at the door. What did Mr. Holmes say were her precise words, Tim?"

"She said we were to 'look to the vicarage!'" said Tim grimly.

"Look to the vicarage? Goodness, can she possibly mean . . . ?" Angela's voice trailed off.

"Whatever she means, Miss Fairfax," observed the marquess, leaning against the mantelshelf, "we cannot afford to disregard any clues, even when they come from an old woman half the population of the valley considers 'dicked in the nob,' as they say!"

"Do you believe she has special powers, Lord Brynne?" Angela pressed.

The marquess looked uncomfortable. "Mr. Holmes sets great store by Granny Meg's powers," he replied evasively. "I do not know whether she is lunatic or magician, but past events testify to her usefulness in divining certain things. She has frequently helped the locals in advising them on what crops to plant, how the coming winter will be, who Johnny Sween will wed, and where Mrs. Cooper lost her wedding ring. You know the sort of thing I mean. But since she has grown so old, many of the locals have begun to doubt her abilities. Seems she's right only the half the time these days."

"But what do *you* think?" asked Angela.

"Standing alone, I do not think I would consider Granny Meg's pronouncement as very significant. But coupled with some other facts... In sum, together Mr. Holmes and I have come to an unfortunate possibility." He eyed her keenly. "Perhaps you have come to the same conclusion."

"Proceed," Angela prompted him warily.

"We believe it possible that Miss Charity Beakman is Harry's mother."

Angela nodded resignedly. "I wondered at the coincidence of her returning to the area just at the precise time Harry appeared at the Abbey. But she's such a timid, innocent little mouse that I could not credit her being the mother of an illegitimate child!"

"So say I, Miss Fairfax," said Tim, a pained look contorting his handsome features. "She's much too pure and young for me to believe such a thing of her, but there is a deal of evidence which—" He broke off, clearly frustrated and unhappy.

"Which implicates her," finished the marquess. "She has been gone for the past eight months." He paused and stared hard at Angela. "May I speak plainly, Miss Fairfax?"

"I should be vastly annoyed if you didn't!" she assured him.

The marquess looked pleased and continued. "If indeed she is Harry's mother, she would have been about six months with child when she left for Portsmouth. Women have been known to hide such a condition even longer than that with the aid of corsets and such."

"And when her aunt died, she did not ask her father to join her in Portsmouth, but handled everything connected with her aunt's funeral alone," said Angela thoughtfully. "I supposed she simply did not want him about, prosing and carrying on as he does, but it could also have been because she had a child and did not want him to know of it!"

"And after her aunt died, she'd no recourse but to return to the vicarage," said the marquess, "but dared not with a babe in tow! Her aunt's servant, the one who disembarked at Keswick, could have taken Harry with her then and brought him round to the Abbey that afternoon, according to Miss Beakman's instructions."

"Yes," agreed Angela. "That's just what someone in her situation might do! With such a father as the vicar, I know I should be frightened to death to tell him about Harry! Poor dear girl!"

"You speak as though there's no possibility of error," Tim broke in rather bitterly. "I still find it hard to believe Miss Beakman the mother of a child out of wedlock! Which brings us to the question of the father. Where is he? Who is he? And why has he deserted her?"

"She might have been forced," Angela suggested reluctantly. "And too ashamed to tell anyone."

The possibility that Charity might have been forcefully ravished seemed to be an even more disturbing and abhorrent possibility to Sir Timothy. His hands clenched the arms of the chair he sat in until his knuckles turned white. "But what about the note? I read it myself, and it was not the hand or the expressions of an educated person. And Miss Beakman is educated!''

''Someone might have penned it for her for a paltry sum, no questions asked,'' said Lord Brynne. ''Or she could have managed it herself. In fact it would seem the logical thing to do, leading us to look in the wrong direction entirely.''

Sir Timothy was silenced and sat scowling down at his boots. Angela felt nearly as blue-devilled as he looked, but she couldn't disagree with the profusion of evidence pointing to Miss Beakman.

''Now the problem remaining, of course, is how to find out for certain,'' said the marquess. ''I'm convinced that asking her outright would be a mistake. If we're wrong in our assumptions, it would be the worst possible insult to Miss Beakman. What do you suggest, Miss Fairfax?''

''We had better proceed slowly and cautiously. I meant to spend some time with Miss Beakman even before this possibility arose. Perhaps the vicar would not object if I tried to become friends with her.''

''Yes, he did seem to like you, Miss Fairfax,'' agreed the marquess, a rueful edge to his voice. ''No doubt the good vicar is drawn to your angelic countenance.''

Angela's face warmed as she remembered her conduct of the night before. Perhaps Lord Brynne made a mental distinction between her angelic looks and her less than angelic behaviour.

Striving to recover her composure, she said, "If I discuss Harry's plight with her, she might betray herself. I'm persuaded that no mother could give up her child without suffering dreadfully. In the meantime, Harry will be perfectly comfortable with us."

Suddenly there was a knock at the door and Mr. Holmes entered the room, followed closely by Fran, who was carrying Harry's basket. Zeus bounded in just behind them. It was obvious by the look on Fran's face and the way Zeus was frisking and whining that something was amiss.

"What's the matter?" demanded the marquess, pushing away from the mantel and standing before them. Zeus sat down at his master's feet and positioned himself just under his lordship's hand, ready for a petting. The large dog panted heavily, but Lord Brynne's gentle stroking of the animal's head seemed to calm him down.

"We was down by the beck, m'lord," Fran haltingly explained. "Harry was sleepin' in 'is basket under the tree, and Mr. Ned was helpin' me look in the shallow water fer some pretty rocks. Sudden-like, I heared Zeus barkin'..."

"Is Harry all right?" Angela stood up and moved closer to peer into the basket, alarm wringing her heart. But Harry was fast asleep, his thumb in his mouth.

"As you kin see, miss, Harry's fine," said Fran. "But in that wee bit o' time I left 'im by the tree, someone come near 'im!"

"Show them the note, Fran," instructed Mr. Holmes.

"Good God, not another note!" expostulated the marquess.

Fran looked reluctant as she produced a piece of paper from her apron pocket. Lord Brynne snatched it from her and hastily read it. "Another warning from the cowardly chap who'll not show his face! It says, 'This is my last warning. Discontinue your search for Harry's mother or suffer the consequences.' Devilish unclear, isn't he? What the deuce does he mean?"

"You don't suppose he'd harm the child, do you?" asked Angela. "I shudder to think this villainous person was so near to Harry. Where was Zeus?"

"Down by the stream with us," confessed Fran, looking miserable. "I put 'im under the tree, Miss Fairfax, t'git 'im out o' the sun," she further explained, her honest, freckled face pale and drawn. "I never thought as 'ow someone might come near the babe, and we was only a few feet away!"

"We don't blame you, Fran," growled Lord Brynne, crushing the note in a clenched fist. "By God, if people under my protection aren't even safe on my own grounds...!"

"Fran didn't want to tell you about the note, m'lord," Mr. Holmes disclosed in his sober way, flinching a little as Fran threw him a resentful glare.

"Whyever not, Fran?" exclaimed Angela.

Fran turned bright red, bowed her head and shuffled her feet.

"Yes, Fran," prompted the marquess. "Why wouldn't you want us to read the note?"

"Well, m'lord," she said meekly. "I...I was afeared you'd s-send Harry away!" She lifted her face, her eyes full of supplication. "I *do* so wish you'd keep 'im! I'm uncommon attached to 'im!"

"As are we all," said Lord Brynne gently. "But you must never keep anything from us pertaining to Harry. Do you understand, Fran?"

"Yes, m'lord" was Fran's muffled response.

Then, as if he knew he were being talked about, Harry squirmed in his basket, gave an extravagant yawn, blinked his eyes open and smiled. He looked as though he appreciated the attention of so many people and considered it his due. Zeus poked his nose into the basket and gave the baby an affectionate lick on his fine head of wispy yellow hair.

"Lor', Zeus! Don't be slobberin' on little Harry like that," scolded Fran.

"Better take him upstairs, Fran," ordered the marquess. "And from now on, if you've a mind to take Harry on an outing, have one of the footmen accompany you. And never, ever leave the child unattended. Is that clear?"

Fran nodded. After she left with Harry and Zeus, Mr. Holmes remarked, "I don't think the baby especially resembles Miss Beakman, do you?"

"Eye and hair colour can change dramatically in the first year or two of life, Mr. Holmes," said the marquess. "We can't judge by appearances at this point. I'm glad you came back. You should know we've been discussing the problem, and Miss Fairfax has suggested that we try to discover by Miss Beakman's behaviour and conversation if there is something to our suspicions. In the meantime, we must watch Harry closely. And do keep a general look-out on all the goings-on about the estate and village. Let me know if you hear or see anything further which might help us. And thank you for your invaluable help thus far.''

Mr. Holmes nodded soberly and took his leave. ''Yes, Mr. Holmes,'' said Tim bitterly, as the door shut behind the steward. ''A thousand thanks for pointing the finger right straight at poor Miss Beakman!''

''Sir Timothy, pray don't be so hard on Mr. Holmes,'' said Angela in a reasoning voice. ''He was only doing as he was asked. And we must come to the bottom of this problem as quickly as possible, for Harry's sake and for his poor mama's sake, too, whoever she is!''

Angela observed that her bracing words hadn't the slightest effect on Sir Timothy. He continued to sit in sulky silence, his arms folded stubbornly across his chest, thoroughly crushing his neckcloth in a total disregard for vanity. This bespoke quite an unsettled mind, in her opinion. But it struck her that he seemed more upset over Miss Beakman's possible guilt than his relationship to her warranted. They hadn't even spoken during the vicar's visit yesterday. In fact, she remembered suddenly, the vicar had levelled one or two looks at Sir Tim which clearly suggested a rooted dislike of the young man.

PLAY "LUCKY HEARTS" AND YOU COULD GET...

★ Exciting Harlequin Regency Romance™ novels—FREE

★ A 20″ Necklace—FREE

★ A surprise mystery gift that will delight you—FREE

THEN CONTINUE YOUR LUCKY STREAK WITH A SWEETHEART OF A DEAL

When you return the postcard on the opposite page, we'll send you the books and gifts you qualify for, absolutely free! Then you'll get 4 new Harlequin Regency Romance™ novels every other month, delivered right to your door. If you decide to keep them, you'll pay only $2.69* per book—that's a saving of 30¢ off the cover price. And there's no extra charge for postage and handling! You can cancel at any time by marking "cancel" on your statement or returning a shipment to us at our cost.

Free Newsletter!

You'll get a free newsletter—an insider's look at our most popular authors and their upcoming novels.

Special Extras—Free!

When you subscribe to the Harlequin Reader Service®, you'll also get additional free gifts from time to time as a token of our appreciation for being a home subscriber.

You'll look like a million dollars when you wear this elegant necklace! It's a generous 20 inches long and each link is double-soldered for strength and durability.

DETACH AND MAIL CARD TODAY

HARLEQUIN "NO RISK" GUARANTEE

★ You're not required to buy a single book—ever!
★ As a subscriber, you must be completely satisfied or you may cancel at any time by marking "cancel" on your statement or returning a shipment of books at our cost.
★ The free books and gifts you receive from this LUCKY HEARTS offer remain yours to keep—in any case.

If offer card is missing, write to:
Harlequin Reader Service, 3010 Walden Ave., P.O. Box 1867, Buffalo, NY 14269-1867

"Sir Timothy, how well do you know Miss Beakman?" she asked him, her curiosity getting the better of her.

Tim looked flustered by the question and did not reply. Just as she was about to repeat herself, Lord Brynne spoke up.

"Miss Fairfax," he began, moving in front of her to sit on the edge of the desk. He propped himself with his arms and crossed his long, sleekly pantalooned legs at the ankles. Angela's eyes involuntarily travelled the full length of his disturbingly masculine form, from the tips of his black, gleaming boots, up and along the lean, taut line of his thighs, past his broad chest encased in a dashing pin-striped waistcoat and finally locked with an intense blue gaze.

"Yes, my lord?" she said in a small voice, mesmerized by the unwilling attraction she felt for this rakish nobleman.

"Why don't you go over to the vicarage at once? I shall have Lawrence order you the cabriolet, and send one of my burliest footmen to stand on the platform behind. I would go with you myself, but I think the vicar will be much more willing to allow Charity to go with you if I'm not along. And Miss Beakman will not be able to confide in you unless you're quite alone. Can you drive a gig, Miss Fairfax?"

"Y-yes," said Angela, swept along by the marquess's commanding personality.

"If you decide to walk with Miss Beakman, don't be surprised or annoyed to discover yourself being followed, because I am going to instruct the footman to do just that—at a discreet distance, of course. With this ridiculous note-writer wandering about, we can't be too careful. Once you have her alone, perhaps you can gain her confidence, or ferret out some useful information. There, what do you say to my plan?''

Angela found herself responding to the marquess's persuasive voice and the compelling gleam in his eyes. ''I'll go, of course. I hadn't ought to be sitting here like a great dolt, had I? I'll just go upstairs and get my pelisse and bonnet and leave immediately!'' She stood up and moved to the door.

''Good afternoon, Miss Fairfax,'' he called, saluting her with a brisk wave of his hand and a flash of even white teeth. ''I fancy we shall have a great deal to discuss when you return!''

Angela smiled back rather uncertainly, suddenly struck with an odd impression of having been sent on a mission for the government. Moments later, in the hall, she remembered her curiosity concerning Tim's degree of acquaintance with Miss Beakman and realized that she had been quite skilfully shuttled out of the room before she could ask any more questions.

Smiling wryly at her image in the mirror as she tied the satin bonnet strings beneath her chin, she said, ''You have won this skirmish, my lord, but I shall not be so cleverly distracted from my objective again! I care not how devastatingly handsome you are!''

WHEN SYDNEY RETURNED to the library after instructing Lawrence concerning his wishes regarding Miss Fairfax and the cabriolet, he discovered that Tim had not moved a muscle. But while his arms were still crossed and his feet positioned just as before on the carpet in front of his chair, his look of angry disbelief had been replaced by one of woeful resignation.

Sydney sat down behind his desk, steepled his long fingers together and lightly rested them against his chin. He peered at his friend and said, "Well, Tim, I wonder how well you *do* know Miss Beakman!"

Tim jerked to attention. His eyes sparkled dangerously as he returned his friend's gaze. "What exactly do you mean by that, Syd? Are you implying that I'm Harry's father? Do you think so little of me that you could think that I would desert Miss Beakman in such a shabby manner? Or that I would write such hateful letters to you?"

"Calm down, Tim, and I will tell you what I think. We are friends, are we not? Will you hear me out?"

Tim pulled a trembling hand through his brown wavy hair, took a deep breath and said wearily, "I will listen, Syd. But you can't expect me to like everything you say."

Sydney nodded his concession to this point and began. "One or two possibilities present themselves to me. First, you and Miss Beakman could have conceived the child together and she never told you about it. You were unaware of her pregnancy, and are therefore not guilty of abandoning anyone." He raised his brows.

"You can dish that theory, Syd. I've never made love to Miss Beakman in my life," said Tim haughtily, obviously highly insulted.

Sydney nodded. "I believe you, so you needn't get up on your high horse. I had to ask. I had to know the degree of your former friendship. Now for my next theory. Wasn't it August of last year that you were found by the vicar at the boat-house with Miss Beakman?"

Tim blinked and cast his eyes about the room, trying to remember. "I don't know! What does it matter? I only kissed her! Let me see, I believe it *was* a year ago August.... The Pembertons were just on the point of returning to London for the Little Season. What does it signify, Syd?"

Sydney grimaced. "If Harry is approximately five months of age, he would have been conceived in August of last year, a fact which might signify a great deal!"

Tim laughed nervously. "Unless my education has been sadly misdirected, it takes a great deal more to put a bun in the oven than mere kissing! No matter how angelic the mother, Syd, there has been, and will only be, one virginal conception written down the annals of history! Even your heavenly houseguest, Miss Fairfax, will have need of more than a chaste kiss to launch the both of you into parenthood!"

"My God, Tim, you run away with yourself!" exclaimed Sydney bitingly. "I've no intention of launching anyone, least of all Miss Fairfax, into parenthood! I don't intend to marry again, as well you know! What can you be thinking of? Let's stick to the main point, if you please!"

Chastened by one of Sydney's rare setdowns, Tim retreated into petulant silence. Sydney, in the meantime, was trying desperately to clear his mind of the unwelcome images Tim's hasty words had created. He saw himself progressing from the aforementioned chaste kiss to a tangle of arms and legs—his arms and legs, and, yes, Angela Fairfax's fair, lithesome arms and legs. His entire being ached with desire as he briefly indulged in this vivid body poem, then twisted with longing when he visualized the logical result of such a passionate tangle: Miss Fairfax pregnant, Miss Fairfax's flat stomach rounded and her small breasts swollen with mother's milk.

Sydney shook himself violently, which drew Tim's rapt attention, and pressed on. "Where was I? Ah, yes. We have established that Miss Beakman may have conceived during the selfsame month you were found together in the boat-house."

"Kissing," Tim pointed out. "Merely kissing!"

"That is what she said you had been doing. That is what she told her papa!" Sydney clarified with a significant nod of his head.

"So?" Tim fairly shouted.

"So, do you remember what happened, Tim? I'm quite sure you don't, because you were too cup-shot to remember! Do you think it possible that Miss Beakman, seeking to shield you from her father's wrath, lied to him about the extent of your intimacies?"

Tim's mouth fell open and his eyes fairly popped from their sockets. "Lord, Syd, do you think . . . ? In the boat-house? Is it possible?"

Sydney shrugged. "Anything is possible."

Tim groaned and buried his face in his hands. "Oh, if I've put that darling girl through torture just because I could not curb my drunken passions! What shall I do, Syd?"

Tim lifted his stricken face to his friend. Considerably moved by the extent of Tim's remorse, Lord Brynne soothed, "Don't repine so, Tim. All of this is conjecture, you know. We don't know anything positive yet. We don't even know if Miss Beakman is the mother."

"But everything is pointing in that direction. And if truth be told," he added emphatically, "I had rather know that I was the father than any other man that walks the earth!"

"You do love her, don't you?" Sydney quietly suggested.

"Yes," Tim replied simply.

"Then why have you done nothing about it, for God's sake?"

Tim shrugged and looked sheepish. "I don't know. Perhaps I thought I had not done with sowing my wild oats. Her father hates me. Maybe I believed I wasn't good enough for her."

Sydney sighed. "I haven't been a good influence on you, have I?"

"You made me see the folly of my drinking," Tim said, rushing to his friend's defence. "If not for you I'd probably be dead in some London gutter by now. I've been stone sober for months now."

"But I never stopped you from wenching!"

"Wenching never gave me a memory loss or caused me to cast up my accounts! Come to think of it, though, one fair maid sent me on a three days' repairing lease!"

They laughed together, easing a little of the tension that had been building up all day. Presently Sydney said, "What will you do?"

Tim promptly replied, "I'm going to marry her, whether she's Harry's mother or not. I'm ready to tie the nuptial knot, Syd!"

Sydney hesitated, but felt duty-bound to suggest another possibility. "What if she *is* Harry's mother, but you're not his father?"

Tim sobered. "I don't know, Syd. I just don't know. And now I have a question for you."

Sydney raised his brows and waited.

"If I'm Harry's father, who's been writing those damned notes?"

"Hmm..." said Sydney. "You have me there, Tim!"

CHAPTER SIX

LORD BRYNNE'S CABRIOLET was a small, elegant carriage, very light and springy. The horse attached to it was a beauty of a high-stepper, and exactly the same pale shade of grey as the carriage. Altogether it was an impressive rig, and like nothing Angela had ever driven before. Sitting straight and pert in the seat, with the brisk autumn air cooling her cheeks to a delicate bloom, Angela was enjoying her short jaunt to the vicarage immensely.

Any gentleman watching her tool down the road might have sighed at the fetching picture she made. Everything about it was so light and elegant—except, of course, for the burly footman balanced on the narrow platform at the back of the carriage. Obviously, for more pleasing proportions, a small-statured tiger in a striped waistcoat ought to have been attending the lady. But Lord Brynne had seemed much more concerned with ensuring her perfect safety than with creating a picture-perfect image. In this instance, Angela completely agreed and was grateful to him.

She was also grateful to Lord Brynne for trusting her with his cattle and carriage. He took her word for it that she could handle the gig and let her go without a lot of instructions and admonitions. And since her papa had fallen asleep on the sofa, she hadn't been required to ask his permission, and was therefore spared a lecture on road safety, which would have lasted a quarter-hour at the least.

Lawrence had obligingly given her directions to the vicarage, and Angela felt quite sure nothing could be simpler to understand. The only difficult part she could foresee was convincing the vicar that Charity ought to be allowed to ride out with her. Despite Charity's obvious capabilities and her extended absence from the vicarage, her father seemed still to be rather over-protective. And if she did get her alone, how was Angela to wring out a confession from the shy, and probably extremely frightened, girl?

Angela thought hard for a minute or two, but was shortly beguiled away from her sober reflections by the pungent, fruity smell of harvest in the air. Colourful leaves cart-wheeled across the road at the whim of breezes which swirled up from the beck below. Autumn was absolutely her favourite time of year, and in the Lake District it quite stole her breath away.

For the moment she was content to let the worries and frets of the day ease away as if by the magic of the Little People. She wondered, rather idly, if Lord Brynne believed in the Little People. However, she still wasn't sure whether he believed in ghosts. His teasing manner when he spoke of Spindle-shanks and Willy left his listener wondering how seriously he took his own stories! She suspected that he told them merely for the sake of entertainment. But what about Granny

Meg? He must believe in a little bit of magic if he were willing to consider seriously the local soothsayer's suggestion that they look to the vicarage.

Now the lane turned and an expansive view of Lake Derwentwater struck her forcefully. The sun was high and the still water faithfully reflected back the jewel-like blue of the cloudless sky. After two more crooks in the road, there was the vicarage, the grassy grave-yard and chapel next to it surrounded by a low rock wall covered with ivy. The vicarage itself was of a moderate size, and was rather newer than most she'd seen, with windows and gables in the Georgian style.

She neatly halted the horse and carriage by the cobbled walkway which twined through a patch of rose bushes on the way to the front door. Simon, the burly footman, hopped down from his perch at the back of the carriage and walked round to hold the horse's leads while Angela paid her visit. She gave the brass knocker a hearty swing and tucked back a flyaway curl as she waited for someone to answer the door.

It was opened by a tall, lean fellow in black coat and trousers, clearly a servant of sorts. Since there was no trace of grey in the man's dark hair, Angela supposed he could not be more than forty years old. However, his angular face was pale and haggard, his expression grim and unfriendly. This had to be Joseph, the groom whom Lord Brynne had described so aptly as looking like a gravedigger! He evidently served Vicar Beak-man as an all-round servant with various duties.

"Good day," said Angela, smiling determinedly. "Is your mistress at home?"

The man did not return Angela's smile. "Who is calling, please?" he coldly enquired.

"Miss Fairfax."

Since the pronouncement of her name did not seem to impress the servant, or, indeed, inspire him to admit her to the house, Angela added, "Miss Beakman is expecting me. I am a visitor in the neighbourhood. I do not have a card with me, or else I'd send one in to her. I grow chilly standing here," she finished pointedly.

Angela had told a little farradiddle, to be sure. In fact, she'd told three. She had calling cards tucked away in her reticule, but she dared not allow Charity the opportunity to refuse her. Charity was certainly not expecting her, and she was not in the least chilly. But though these were several whiskers in a row, Angela felt fairly confident that she would not be sent directly to Hell for lying without at least an opportunity to explain herself.

The man nodded, rather reluctantly Angela thought, and led her down a short hallway and into what appeared to be the parlour. Charity was sitting in a rocking-chair near the fire and was busily employed in some sort of stitchery.

At the sound of the door opening, Charity looked up and stared wide-eyed and open-mouthed as Angela walked into the room. Before the startled girl could betray at least one of her untruths to the servant, Angela exclaimed, "Miss Beakman! How are you? Here I am, just as I promised! I do hope I have not kept you waiting?"

Angela was relieved to discover that although Charity was painfully shy, she wasn't a slowtop. Understanding flickered in her soft brown eyes and she said, "No, I have been much occupied, as you see. Do come in, Miss Fairfax, and sit by the fire."

Angela sat down in a chair opposite Charity. As she arranged her skirts, she glanced up and saw Joseph still hovering at the doorway. "Thank you, Joseph," said Charity dismissively, but with a nervous little flutter of her hands. "And do close the door behind you so we may keep the heat of our fire."

Joseph looked sour and did not seem well pleased to have been sent away. Angela thought it singular for the servant to be so encroaching, and quite odd that Charity felt the need to explain why she wanted the door closed. It occurred to her that the poor girl had not only to deal with an overbearing father, but with pugnacious servants, as well. Timid creatures like Charity seemed to invite that sort of bullying. But then Joseph looked the sort who could bully just about anyone if he chose to, and probably just by staring him or her down.

"You must excuse me for spinning a whisker to your servant, Miss Beakman, but he did seem reluctant to let me in, and I did so wish to see you today!"

Charity had sat down again and was clutching her cloth and embroidery frame against her chest like a shield. "Oh!" she said, with another nervous flutter of her hands. "Pay no heed to Joseph! I am so pleased to see you!" She bowed her head shyly.

Angela wasn't completely sure that Charity was pleased to see her, but she was determined to put the girl at ease. "After we met yesterday, I thought I should like to get to know you better. I'm persuaded that we're near the same age."

"Yes, I suppose we are!" she replied, lifting her eyes briefly to Angela's face. Angela smiled reassuringly and was rewarded by a fleeting, uncertain smile from Charity.

"Are you settled in after your long journey from Portsmouth? You must be tired!" She watched the girl for some sign of agitation connected with the subject of Portsmouth.

"No, I am quite well, thank you." Charity resumed her needlework.

Angela wracked her brain for some commonplace remark before daring to ask her to leave the house with her, and said, "What are you sewing, Miss Beakman? Is it a tablecloth?"

"No, it's an altar cloth. Another is needed for the chapel." Then she unexpectedly lifted her head and added confidingly, "The other is so shabby. It quite wrung my heart to see it so tattered when I returned from Portsmouth! I hope to get this one done before Sunday services."

Angela stared at Charity, uncertainty seizing her. Sitting in this quiet parlour, while Charity sewed on an altar cloth, she began to think their suspicions rather ludicrous. Charity looked so sweet and devout with her head bent over her saintly task. Her brown curls were tucked up into a tidy knot and she wore a demure round gown of pale yellow cambric.

"Where do you come from, Miss Fairfax?"

Angela was surprised by the question, having assumed that she would be required to guide and prod the conversation along without any help from Charity.

"Will you call me Angela?" Suddenly Angela wanted to befriend the shy girl, whether she was Harry's mother or not.

Charity seemed surprised and touched. "Why, yes. If you will call me Charity," she replied softly.

"Well, Charity, I'm from Sussex," said Angela. "Why don't you come for a ride with me in Lord Brynne's splendid cabriolet and I'll tell you all about my home in Finchingfield. Rather a dull business, really, but you'll love the marquess's rig! And it's such a beautiful day!"

Charity looked distressed. "I don't know.... That is, my father may not wish me to. What I mean is, I..."

"Don't bother to explain, Charity," said Angela kindly. "I think I understand. Lord Brynne is known to be a rake, though he deports himself tolerably well hereabouts. And you are worried that as one of Lord Brynne's guests, I may not be acceptable to your father?"

Charity nodded miserably.

"But it can't do any harm to ask, can it? Where is the vicar?"

"In his library." A flicker of hope dawned in Charity's brown eyes. "He did seem to like you, Angela. Perhaps he *will* let me go! Wait here, I shall be back directly!"

Angela did not have to wait long. In less time than it takes to whistle "God Save the King," Charity returned with her father. Vicar Beakman entered the room smiling, a circumstance that boded well, but then Sir Timothy was not nearby to annoy him.

"Miss Fairfax, how pleasant to see you again!" he said cheerfully. "I did not know you meant to pay us a visit today."

"Dear me, I thought I mentioned it! What a sad scatterbrain I am! And I even thought I'd asked your permission to take Charity on a drive with me. Your countryside is so magnificent, Vicar Beakman, that I find I can't see enough of it! You would be doing me the greatest service if you were to allow Charity to accompany me and point out some of the local spots of interest."

Angela said all this in a great hurry and with such a persistent smile and joyful attitude that she felt the vicar would have to be a brute to deny her. And with Charity standing there so meekly, her eyes fairly misted with hope, how could he refuse?

The vicar raised a brow. Angela thought his small black eyes were set rather too close together in his wide face, but then it could have been the largeness of his nose which made them look that way. He was dressed all in black again, with the grey neckcloth the only relief against the unremitting soberness of his attire.

"You are come alone, Miss Fairfax?" he enquired at length. "Lord Brynne did not insist on showing you the sights himself? Perhaps one of his, er, guests has accompanied you?" His eyes strayed towards the window facing the front of the house.

Angela recognized the vicar's concern that the marquess or Tim might be waiting outside. "No, I am quite alone! And if you're thinking that my papa is a sad excuse for a guardian, you have only to come outside and see the giant of a footman who has been sent along to protect me! We will be quite safe. I'm a tolerable whipster, too, and do not try to drive to an inch, or any such nonsense."

Vicar Beakman's small eyes crinkled into raisins and his thin lips curved upward in a smile. "You seem a good, as well as a pretty, girl, Miss Fairfax. I can't help but wonder how you came to be acquainted with Lord Brynne." His smile slowly took leave of his face as he waited for her answer.

Angela forced a carefree laugh. "Vicar Beakman, I'm sure you'll think I'm much too coming to speak so plainly, but I must. I know Lord Brynne is a reputed rake and you cannot like him. But I assure you that he, and his friend, Sir Timothy, have been perfect gentlemen and I am not the least worried about my virtue while visiting at Castlerigg Abbey."

"What about your reputation?"

"With my father constantly about and his lordship's own mother playing hostess, one would have to be an absolute addlepate to suspect mischief where there is none!"

Undoubtedly concerned lest he be lumped into the unflattering category of "addlepate," Vicar Beakman relented at last. "Yes, 'tis true that Lady Brynne's as well as your own father's presence at the Abbey lends respectability to your visit. You may go, Charity. Fetch your bonnet and pelisse."

Charity did not say a word, but hastened out of the room to do as she was bid. "Vicar Beakman, you have my profuse thanks!" said Angela, breathing a sigh of relief and extending her hand.

Vicar Beakman took her hand and held it firmly between his two. "I only make one stipulation, Miss Fairfax," he told her, seizing her hand and pulling her closer as if wishing to impart a secret.

"Yes, sir?" she said, a little alarmed to find herself not six inches away from the vicar's black bombazine waistcoat. She tried to pull free her hand, but he held it fast. "W-what is your stipulation, sir?" she prompted him.

His black, currantlike eyes bore into her. Once again Angela felt remarkably like a plump apple tart, or something equally as luscious, for the vicar looked dreadfully hungry. In the space of a moment, however, the hungry look passed and he grew quite serious. "Even though Lady Brynne is currently residing at the Abbey, I still do not wish Charity to go there without me," he told her. "Do not take her there under any inducement, Miss Fairfax."

Angela laughed nervously, wondering what inducement he could be thinking of. "Certainly, if you do not wish me to, I shall not!" She pulled free and stepped back, her breath suspended.

The vicar smiled again, but this time his eyes did not crinkle. "Nevertheless, since my wife has passed on to that more noble abode—" his eyes flickered heavenwards "—I am solely responsible for Charity's well-being and reputation."

"I'm ready, Miss Fairfax!"

Angela turned gratefully at the sound of Charity's happy voice. She was dressed in a fawn-coloured pelisse and bonnet, not exactly in the latest mode of fashion, but she looked very pretty. Certainly happiness at the prospect of an afternoon away from the vicarage must have accounted for the sparkle in her eye and her light step as she crossed the room.

"Be back by three, Charity," instructed her father. "I leave for Keswick at cock-crow tomorrow and must take to my bed early tonight; therefore, we shall dine at four." Then he stooped to offer his cheek for a kiss. Charity did not look especially delighted by the invitation, but obediently gave her father a quick peck on his jaw, assured him that she would be punctual and scurried out the door. Angela politely bade the vicar goodbye, taking care not to give him her hand this time, and quickly followed Charity.

Angela wisely kept their conversation to general topics at first, but at the same time she felt she was coming to know Charity a little better. Presently the shy girl grew more comfortable with Angela and was coaxed into saying a few harmless sentences.

Chatting and guiding the horse along the lane, Angela calculated how long it might take her to win Charity's confidence, and wondered when the vicar would return from Keswick the following day. If another visit proved necessary on the morrow, she would make certain that she came when the vicar was not about, thereby gaining more time alone with Charity. But rather than asking Charity directly when she might expect to find her father away from the house, she said, in what she hoped was an offhand manner, "Does your father go often to Keswick? Has he business there?"

"He visits the foundling home once a week," replied Charity, the relaxed, upward tilt of her mouth drooping suddenly.

"How very kind of him!" said Angela, wondering at Charity's sudden dejection. Surely she did not miss her pompous father when he left her alone at the vicarage! "Does he stay the whole day?"

"Yes," Charity replied, but changed the subject immediately. Angela was a little bewildered by Charity's reluctance to speak of her father's clerical duties, but having discovered what she wanted to know, she let the subject drop.

They kept to the lanes which bordered the lake as they tooled along. Angela bided her time and waited for a propitious moment to bring up the subject of Harry. She did not want to rush the business and make Charity suspicious of her.

By and by Charity's spirits revived from the sudden melancholy and she seemed greatly to enjoy the beautiful countryside, especially the sight of the geese and other wildfowl which congregated in the shallow marshes near the lakeshore. The breeze grew rather brisker as a pleasant hour passed, and they spied three or four small sailing vessels on the water, skimming along at a good clip.

"I should love to go boating again one day," Charity said, looking wistful. "The last time I was on the water was at Lady Pemberton's lawn party. Before the dancing, you see, we all spent the day out of doors, walking, playing croquet and boating. It was lovely!"

Encouraged by this first bit of conversation which progressed beyond the weather and the scenery, Angela said excitedly, "Lord Brynne has a boat! In fact, he must have several boats! I heard him talking the other night with Sir Timothy about jibs and rudders and booms and the like. I believe those are nautical terms, are they not? Anyway, perhaps they would be willing to take us out on a little sailing expedition."

Charity's eyes grew enormous. "Indeed, Angela, you must know my father would never permit me to go!" Then, blushing furiously, "And even if Papa gave his permission, I do not think I should like it!"

"Goodness, you aren't afraid of Lord Brynne, are you? I know he has a wretched reputation, but he's behaved very well towards me." Her brow winkled in thought. "I think he must have imposed some sort of rakish code of honour upon himself which allows him to dally with only a certain type of woman!"

Blushing even more profusely, Charity hurriedly explained, "Oh, no! 'Tis not his lordship I wish to avoid!'' Then, seeming to realize she'd said a tad too much, she fell silent.

"Then it is Sir Timothy's company you wish to shun?" suggested Charity, dropping her hands so that the horse slowed to a walk.

"Pray, how did I give you such a false impression?" replied Charity, lifting her small face and putting on a brave, though slightly tremulous, smile. "I only wish to obey my father."

"But you must be itching for a little jollification, as my brothers always say. Tending your sick aunt for so long, you are due for a little fun, I'd say!"

Charity did not reply and looked as if she were about to burst into tears. Alarmed at such a strong reaction to her gentle prodding, Angela did not press her further.

Just then Angela recognized the road leading to the George and Vulture. She turned her horse's leads and was soon passing that establishment, making for Castlerigg Circle. Charity raised no objection as Angela reined in at the bottom of the hill and handed the ribbons to Simon, who'd bounded down as soon as the carriage drew to a halt, ready to assist the ladies from the carriage and mind the horse.

"Come, Charity, let's walk!" said Angela, smiling kindly.

Charity returned a rather watery smile and allowed Simon to hand her down from the carriage.

Slipping her arm into Charity's, Angela walked them up the hill and around and through the stones, repeating the story Lord Brynne had told her about the

Circle and coaxing Charity to enlarge on his information if she could. Charity didn't have much else to say about the Circle, but the change of subject and scenery seemed to improve her despondent mood. Indeed, the girl went from happy to sad and back again with the regularity of a metronome!

Presently they sat down on a flat rock near the base of one of the towering stones. Angela determined to try one more approach: a direct one. If she were going to find out something, she had better do so now. She had observed her watch locket earlier and knew it was nearing three o'clock.

"Mysteries, like this wonderful old pagan ruin, are fascinating, aren't they? Though there are some mysteries I'd as lief do without!" she began.

Charity turned her head to look intently at Angela. "What do you mean?"

"Take this business with little Harry!" Angela plunged on, avoiding catching Charity's eye. "I do so wish we knew who the child's mother is. He's such a darling boy, I don't know how anyone could give him up!"

After rather a lengthy pause, and just as Angela was about to speak again, Charity quietly said, "Perhaps the mother thinks he will be better off with Lord Brynne. Perhaps she can't give him a proper home, or does not wish to bring shame on his head or on herself."

"Oh, but I do not know if his lordship will keep him! Certainly, if he gives him away, it will be to good people, but possibly far from here! But I've the strongest notion that a child ought to be with his mother,'' Angela declared, darting Charity a quick glance. "What do you think, Charity?''

"I d-dare not hazard an opinion on something I know n-nothing about,'' faltered Charity, standing abruptly. "Miss Fairfax, er, that is, Angela, would you be so kind as to take me home now? I have the most dreadful headache!''

Charity did look as though she were suffering from some sort of affliction, but Angela was willing to wager that it wasn't the headache. She could imagine the conflicting emotions warring in the girl's heart, if indeed the child were hers. But if she wasn't pining over her child and agonizing and questioning her decision to abandon him—if he wasn't her child at all—there was certainly *something* bothering Charity Beakman. And Angela had a strong suspicion that it all had to do with Sir Timothy Clives.

A HEARTY GALLOP about the estate was just what he'd needed, thought Sydney as he strode towards the house, smiling. There was nothing like the rush of wind in your hair, the thunder of hooves against the hard earth, and a magnificent animal beneath you to make you forget a female, even if, as in this case, the female was such a taking little puss. But now he had quite dismissed her from his mind. As he combed his fingers through his disordered hair, he wondered what Mrs. Hobbs had planned for dinner.

Suddenly Sydney's calm was destroyed. Or perhaps he realized that he hadn't attained a state of calm at all. Coming up the drive in the cabriolet was Miss Fairfax, her tiny gloved hands handling the ribbons with expert ease. He reached the gravelled drive just as she pulled in front of the house. Stepping forward, as common politeness dictated he must, he helped her down from the seat.

"Lord Brynne, I'm so glad to have encountered you," said Miss Fairfax in a great rush. Her hair had escaped her bonnet in more than one place and the yellow curls framed her wind-kissed cheeks quite charmingly. What an angel she was!

Then she glanced down at her hand, which he still held quite unnecessarily in his own. Cursing himself for an absolute clod-pole, he released her hand and tried to look completely unaffected by the proximity. In truth, any vestige of sanity his gallop had lent him had fled the minute he'd set eyes on her again. It was a lowering realization.

"Did you make some progress with Miss Beakman?" he asked her as he gave his jacket sleeve a straightening twitch, endeavouring at the same time to suppress his urge to kiss her.

"Perhaps I did. Truth to tell, I don't know! But I have some questions for you!"

His eyes locked on hers. "Questions for me?" Then, feeling a trifle defensive, he said, "You're not beginning to suspect, like half my household, that I'm Harry's father, are you?"

Miss Fairfax made a scolding little sound with her tongue and looked over her shoulder at Simon, who was holding the horse's reigns till a stable-lad could come and take the entire equipage away. Charity gave the marquess a speaking look. "Can we, perhaps, walk in the garden for a minute or two?" she asked him pointedly. "There we can speak privately."

Sydney hesitated. The last thing he wanted was Miss Fairfax all to himself. His eyes wandered over the delicate bones of her face, the berry-red ripeness of her lips. She was too tempting by half, the naughty little angel. How could she look so heavenly, yet be such a temptress?

"My lord?" The seraphic face held a puzzled expression, yet the soft grey eyes seemed too discerning for his own peace of mind. He had a frightening thought that she might recognize the lustful yearnings he barely held in check.

"Of course, if you wish," he acquiesced, offering his arm. Then he steeled himself for the quiver of longing that snaked through him as she slipped her arm in his. By fixing his thoughts on icy mountain streams and frosty winter gales, he managed to keep his composure as they walked the short distance round to the gardens at the side of the house. Once inside the gate, he immediately disengaged himself and offered her a seat in a small copse surrounded by climbing wisteria vines. Growing more leafless by the day as the season progressed, they still provided the privacy Miss Fairfax had requested.

"Now, what did you wish to discuss, Miss Fairfax?" he asked formally.

Miss Fairfax stared up at him, clearly perplexed by his stiff demeanour. "Are you quite the thing, my lord? You look a bit flushed and your eyes seem rather feverish!''

"I feel perfectly splendid," he replied curtly. "Please proceed."

To his chagrin, a look of hurt flitted across her face. He was on the verge of apologizing for his priggish behaviour, blaming it on he knew not what, when he saw a gleam of determination slowly build and replace the pained look in her eyes.

"I want you to tell me everything you know about Sir Timothy and Charity Beakman!" she announced, thrusting out her small, pointed chin. "And I want you to tell me at once!"

Sydney raised his brows, his amusement thankfully overriding his desire for the moment. "And if I don't?" he couldn't resist asking.

"I'll, I'll... Well, you know very well I can't plant you a facer or any such thing, but I think you've been keeping information from me and it makes me feel downright waspish, as Papa would say!"

Sydney sighed and looked rueful. "You're a quick little codling, ain't you? But did it never occur to you that I'm being respectful of your delicate sensibilities by keeping certain things from you, Miss Fairfax?"

"Poppycock, Lord Brynne!" she said scornfully. "Delicate sensibilities have no place in this situation. Please do not treat me like a piece of porcelain!"

"As you wish, Miss Fairfax," he replied, pretending contrition. "And, as you doubtless suspect, Tim and Miss Beakman do have a bit of a history. Actually, I did not mention this to you before because I wasn't sure whether it applied to this hubble-bubble over Harry or not. I'm *still* not sure.''

"Go on," said Angela eagerly.

"There was an incident a year ago August which involved Tim and Miss Beakman, and Lady Pemberton's boat-house!''

Angela digested this silently, seemed to be counting the months back to Harry's possible conception, then squeaked, "Surely not in a boat-house, my lord!''

This drew a reluctant laugh from Sydney. "It has been known to happen in other even less commodious localities, Miss Fairfax.''

"Oh, dear!" was Miss Fairfax's only comment.

Sydney grew sober. "But you must remember that all this is conjecture. Sometimes I fear we may find ourselves considerably embarrassed by our amateur sleuthing.''

Miss Fairfax blinked several times. "Even the boathouse is conjecture?''

"Yes.''

Now she looked really perplexed. "But I don't understand, my lord. You mean Sir Timothy doesn't know whether or not something happened at the boathouse?''

"I'm afraid that's the precise truth of it, Miss Fairfax.''

Obviously, speech was now beyond her power. Miss Fairfax looked incredulous. Certainly nothing she'd read in any book could explain to her such a strange happenstance. Lord Brynne knew Tim's lack of memory must seem deplorable to Miss Fairfax.

"Don't cudgel your brain, my dear," he explained, moved to pity by her stricken look. "Tim had been drinking that night, and that's why he doesn't remember what happened."

Angela's eyes rounded. "Does he always forget what happens to him when he's been drinking?"

"Unfortunately, yes. Perhaps if he drank only a little he would be all right. But Tim can never drink just a little. Once he has got himself started, there's no stopping until he's positively top-heavy. The next day he doesn't remember a thing. Simply said, some people can't drink anything stronger than tea. I've noticed it seems to run in families. His father was the same way. A deuced inconvenient circumstance, wouldn't you say?"

"Indeed," replied Angela, frowning and concentrating on the ground. Then she lifted her eyes to his. "But I think I've noticed that Sir Timothy doesn't drink wine with his dinner, nor have I seen him share a brandy with you and Papa in the evening. Has he quit drinking altogether?"

"Yes, he has," said Sydney, touched by her hopeful, concerned expression.

"Oh, I'm so glad!" she sighed, obviously relieved. "But I do so pity him," she added sympathetically. "He must feel wretched about what has, that is, what *may* have happened. Does he love her?"

"I believe so."

"Then why hasn't he married her, pray?"

"I'm not sure. Perhaps, like many men, he has been afraid to buckle himself to one woman for life. And the vicar has never liked him, even before the incident. Vicar Beakman deplores the sins of the flesh, which, I daresay, encompasses almost all of them.''

"Good heavens, the vicar knows about the, er, boat-house?''

"Miss Beakman told him that Tim merely kissed her. Of course she could have lied to protect him.''

Miss Fairfax pursed her lips reflectively. Once again, his eyes were drawn to that most inviting feature of her face and he groaned inwardly. Firmly shifting his gaze to the fence post, he continued. "It seems only Miss Beakman knows for sure. And I begin to think that only Tim can make her own up to the truth, whatever it may be. The truth about the boat-house, Harry, the night of her return from Portsmouth, everything!''

"Then we must contrive to bring them together, my lord,'' Miss Fairfax said emphatically. She stood up, that familiar look of determination spread over her angelic features, her grey eyes shining.

"Indeed, we must come up with a plan,'' agreed the marquess, bemusedly offering her his arm. "But first we'll have tea, Miss Fairfax. Shall we?''

"A splendid idea, my lord,'' she said, smiling up at him.

Remembering how she had mesmerized him yesterday at the tea-table, her innocent seductiveness bringing him, metaphorically, to his knees, Lord Brynne wasn't sure it was such a splendid idea. But like a doomed man enjoying his last meal, he relished the sweet agony of it, and with a philosophical shrug escorted Miss Fairfax into the house.

CHAPTER SEVEN

SIR TIMOTHY READILY AGREED to the plan which Lord Brynne and Angela had devised to lure Charity out of the vicarage and into their collective company for the following morning. However, he was quite shocked to discover that Angela knew about his propensity for drinking to excess and his possible indiscretion with Charity.

"But as I told him, Miss Fairfax, there was no keeping you out of the thick of things at this point," said Lord Brynne in a low voice as they walked in to dinner together. "And, despite your obvious youth and inexperience, you seem to be awake upon every suit and pluck to the backbone, as well."

Angela had to thank her older brothers for her understanding of cant terms, since she had been obliged to make sense out of their conversation as best she could ever since the eldest had gone away to Eton. "Thank you, my lord," she murmured, with an arch look. "It is gratifying to know that despite the fact that I am a female, you consider I have wit and nerve enough to help you solve the mystery of Harry's abandonment."

Lord Brynne bowed slightly and returned, "Indeed, Miss Fairfax, I must admit that I had doubts about you at the beginning. I supposed that with such an abundance of feminine beauty and charm, Heaven could not dare to bless you with superior intellect, as well." Lord Brynne's deep blue eyes twinkled merrily.

Blushing hotly, she replied, "I wonder you mention it, my lord. Most men do not seem to value wit in a woman."

"Nay, Miss Fairfax, you do not give us enough credit," his lordship replied, pulling out her chair and speaking softly into her ear. "We value wit where we find it, but most beautiful women hide or ignore whatever intelligence they possess, and in the end seem to lose it altogether."

Angela turned to look back at Lord Brynne, intending to defend the female sex and vocally spurn such erroneous ideas about beauty and brains being at odds with each other. But as he was still leaning low over her shoulder, she suddenly found her eyes locked with his and his lips not two inches away. She gasped and discovered herself speechless. At such close quarters, his eyes were so very blue, so very teasing, and so very compelling. And his lips looked so firm and soft and . . . *capable!*

Angela wrenched her eyes away and fixed them upon the plate in front of her. *Capable of what?* she asked herself. *Capable of kissing you senseless,* said her inner voice, which always was so distressingly honest and blunt. Then, as she fumbled with her serviette, she reasoned that she should not be in the least surprised to have noticed that his lips looked capable. What else would they be, pray? He *was* a rake, wasn't he?

Pushing aside her conjectures about the various capabilities required of the average rake, and squelching with fervour the idea that Lord Brynne was very probably more than just average in said capabilities, she ate her dinner without having much to say to anyone. However, as she continued to contemplate rakish capabilities during the first three courses, she blushed a great deal.

When the gentlemen had joined them in the drawing-room after dinner, Lord Brynne sent for Fran and requested that Harry be brought down. The baby was greeted with enthusiasm, and handed round to each person who expressed an interest in bouncing the chubby little cherub upon their knee.

Angela noted that Sir Timothy kept Harry the longest and even looked a bit anxious when the others had their turn at holding him. Now he was enjoying a second turn at holding Harry, and it did not look as though he meant to give him up again to anyone. The mere possibility of Harry being his had evidently inspired him to feel the natural possessiveness of parenthood.

When Harry started fussing, Lord Brynne disappeared and returned with a toy which belonged to Wellesley. He admitted that the plaything, which was a wooden cup on the end of a smoothly carved handle with a ball attached to it by a long string, was probably too advanced for Harry actually to play with, but perhaps they could amuse him a little by demonstrating how the toy was meant to be used.

"I daresay, Syd," said Tim repressively, "he would like it well enough if it fit in his mouth, but since that is *not* the case..."

"Well, we can at least try, can't we?" returned Lord Brynne. The object of the toy was to flip the ball into the air and deposit it in the cup. After only one miss and a shout of deep-timbred laughter, with Zeus barking excitedly at his heels all the while, Lord Brynne succeeded in the task.

"Sydney was always so very dextrous," remarked Lady Brynne in a proud whisper to Angela.

Angela nodded mutely, inclined to believe that in this case the dowager was not stretching the truth to impress her. Dextrous and capable...they meant more or less the same thing, didn't they?

"Here, Tim, you do it," said Lord Brynne, handing the toy to his friend. "You see? Harry likes it."

Harry had indeed ceased fussing. He had either been mesmerized by Lord Brynne's feat, or perhaps merely startled by Zeus's barking. Tim seemed reluctant to hand Harry over to Angela, but the enticement of a challenge was too much for him. At first Tim did not prove quite as adept at the skill, but Lord Brynne tutored him until he was almost as proficient as himself.

When Lord Amesbury was asked if he would like to try his hand at cupping the ball, he sleepily declined, saying to the dowager, "Boys will be boys, eh, my sausage?"

Impatiently waiting her turn, Angela did not think Lord Brynne would invite her to participate. And this omission was based, no doubt, on the assumption that as a delicate female she would not wish to make a spectacle of herself in the drawing-room. She was about to express her indignation at being left out of such a sport simply because she was not wearing trousers, and, furthermore, to declare that she had no compunction about making a spectacle of herself, when Lord Brynne handed her the toy and said, "How rude of me, Miss Fairfax. Ladies ought to be first, oughtn't they?"

"Goodness, Sydney, you don't suppose Miss Fairfax wants to overheat herself in such a manner..." began Lady Brynne.

But Angela swiftly handed Harry to Tim and accepted the toy with alacrity, then hopped about the room trying to cup the ball till she laughed out loud. She conquered the art quickly and soon sat down, her face warm with her exertion and perhaps a little embarrassment.

Unfortunately, now Harry cried in earnest. With nothing left to entertain or alarm him, he threw his chubby arms and legs about and screamed. Fran stepped forward at this point, and as soon as she lifted him from Tim's arms, he quieted.

"By God, Franny," said Sir Timothy admiringly, "you have a hand with babes, don't you?"

"I've lots of experience, sir," Fran said modestly. Then, turning to Lord Brynne, "I'd best get 'im up t' bed, m'lord. Might we go now?" Lord Brynne bade her good-night with a smile, and they left, Zeus following closely behind.

"She's too attached to that child," stated Lady Brynne, as the door closed behind them. "When the mother is finally discovered, you'll have one heartbroken little maid on your hands, Sydney."

"Perhaps she could be hired as Harry's nursemaid," said Tim, on a sudden inspiration.

"Pooh, Tim," demurred the dowager. "That babe's mother could no more afford a nursemaid than she could vacation on the Continent! And his father, no doubt, is some care-for-nobody, kicking up a lark with some other poor girl by now!"

Tim was about to open his mouth to object when he caught Lord Brynne's warning look. Since Lady Brynne and Lord Amesbury had not been included in their discussions, they hadn't the slightest idea that Charity and Tim might be the child's parents. Tim bit his tongue and walked away to stand by the French doors which opened to the balcony overlooking the front lawn and a view of the mountains beyond.

Angela's eyes were drawn to the view, as well. A three-quarter moon shone brightly through a few thin clouds, the countryside lying still and quiet below. There was hardly any wind, but they could make do with just a little breeze for their sails tomorrow, she supposed. Her main fear was that it might rain, because they could never induce Charity to go boating in a thunderstorm, nor would they wish to do such a foolish thing themselves. Since all their plans hinged on that boating expedition, she had to pray for sunshine.

ANGELA'S PRAYERS were answered. A bright midmorning sun shone down on them as she drove Charity along the lakeshore in Lord Brynne's cabriolet. Angela wore a lavender pelisse with a matching bonnet, both trimmed with swansdown. Charity wore her fawn-coloured pelisse and bonnet again and looked just as demure and pretty as before.

It had not been an easy task convincing Charity to join her. No doubt she had alarmed her a little the previous day when she had talked about Harry, but Angela coaxed and begged for her company so engagingly that in the end Charity could not refuse. And, if truth be told, perhaps Charity wanted to go and even secretly wished for an opportunity to unburden herself to someone who would not judge her too harshly.

"Angela, we aren't going to the Abbey, are we?" she presently asked, observing with misgiving the direction in which they were travelling. "You know my father forbade me to go there!"

"Heavens, Charity!" Angela exclaimed with a laugh. "Of course we aren't going to the Abbey! I would never disregard your father's wishes. However, we shall be on his lordship's land for a few minutes. There is a lane bordering the lake just below the

Abbey, which I've been told has a very pretty aspect at this time of year.''

"Do you mean where Lord Brynne docks his boats?'' said Charity, eyeing Angela warily.

"Yes, I suppose his boats are docked there,'' replied Angela nonchalantly. "It would seem the most likely place to dock them, of course, since it is so near the Abbey.''

Charity said no more, but Angela sensed that the girl was becoming suspicious. She flicked her ribbons and urged the horse to a brisker trot, bent on getting on to the next phase of their plan before Charity could insist on being returned to the vicarage.

At last the dock came into view on the right, two sailing dinghies and a larger sailing vessel moored to the posts. Lord Brynne stood looking out across the lake, one hand shielding his eyes from the sun, while a servant appeared to be cleaning out and preparing one of the dinghies for his lordship's use.

"There is Lord Brynne!'' exclaimed Angela, injecting surprise into her voice. "Why, I was sure he was going riding today! Look, he's waving at us. I do believe he wants us to stop, Charity!''

"I don't think my father would approve,'' said Charity in a nervous voice.

"Pooh!'' said Angela dismissively. "He probably only wishes to say good-morning to you. Your father can't object to that! Besides, he's standing in the middle of the road and will be trampled to death if I do not stop!''

Charity could not wish for the marquess to be trampled, and seeming to resign herself to the inevitable, she sat stiffly and stared straight ahead. Angela halted the carriage and Simon ran forward to stand at the horse's head. Then, when Lord Brynne moved to the side of the carriage and smiled up at them, Charity's resistance seemed to melt.

But who could resist him? thought Angela, especially as he looked so well in his sailing toggery. He was dressed casually in white pantaloons which hugged his shapely legs, top boots, a blue kerseymere tailcoat, a striped waistcoat, with a blue neckcloth tied loosely about his neck. His hair was wind-tousled, healthy colour skimmed his high cheek-bones, and his eyes sparkled as blue as the lake behind him. Added to his considerable physical appeal, of course, was his innate charm and the ability he possessed to put people at their ease.

"Miss Fairfax, Miss Beakman, how do you do?" he began, casually leaning against the carriage and resting his booted foot on the step. "Out for another jaunt in the countryside, I see. A beautiful day, is it not?"

Charity nodded agreement and Angela said, "Quite beautiful! But I thought you were going riding, my lord. Changed your mind?"

"I ride throughout the winter, Miss Fairfax, but there are few days left which will be pleasant enough for boating. I decided to take out one of my small boats for an hour or so. Mrs. Hobbs made me a lunch, too. Might even do a little fishing, since I've no one to talk to."

"Where is Sir Timothy?" Angela plunged on shamelessly, fully aware that Charity had stiffened when she heard Tim's name mentioned. "Won't he join you?"

"The idle fellow was asleep when I left the house." Lord Brynne sighed heavily. "I'm afraid *he* won't be joining me!"

"Well, I pity you excessively," returned Angela briskly. "And I'm sure that we would be quite happy to join you if we weren't otherwise occupied." She lifted her hands and gripped the ribbons as if she were prepared to continue their drive.

Lord Brynne's face lit up, as though a brilliant idea had suddenly come to him. Angela had to stifle a giggle. He was performing his part quite well. In fact, he seemed to be enjoying it excessively.

"But you've all day to complete your drive, Miss Fairfax! Couldn't you and Miss Beakman join me in the boat for just an hour? I would not think of keeping you longer. And I would be perfectly willing to wait for Miss Beakman to obtain permission from her father." He smiled up at Charity and raised his brows expectantly.

"Well, *I'm* quite willing to come with you, Lord Brynne. But the decision must be Charity's!" said Angela, idly swatting at a fly.

Charity looked stricken to have the entire weight of the decision placed on her. "My...my father is not at home, Lord Brynne," she faltered. "And he is not expected back till this evening. I'm not able to ask his permission, my lord!"

"Ah!" said Lord Brynne, flicking his hand negligently. "Then you must make your own decision. I do hope you decide in my favour, Miss Beakman. The more I think on it, the more I realize how dashed lonely it will be without someone to bear me company. But I will understand if you prefer to amuse yourself in some other way."

Now Lord Brynne looked up appealingly at Charity. The look of appeal, and his implication that her decision hinged on her desire to seek amusement at the cost of someone else's loneliness, had their effect upon her. "But, my lord, it is not that I wish expressly to go driving in the carriage instead of boating on the lake! Indeed, I *love* to go out on the water above all things. It's just that—"

"Then it is settled, Miss Beakman!" he exclaimed, reaching for her hand to help her down from the carriage. "You have made me very happy!"

Charity automatically gave Lord Brynne her hand and found herself helped down from the carriage, escorted across the lawn and down the dock and seated in the boat in no more than three shakes of a lamb's tail. Angela climbed in beside the dazed girl, just as they'd planned, and Lord Brynne was about to step in behind her when they heard Tim's cry. He was right on cue.

"Hallo! Say, you aren't going without me, are you?" Tim was hurrying down the softly sloping hill from the Abbey, another basket of food swinging from his arm. He was dressed very similarly to Lord

Brynne, but his coat was Manilla brown, nearly the exact shade of is hair.

At the sight and sound of Sir Timothy, Charity clutched the sides of the boat and turned a ghostly white. "Y-you s-said, S-Sir Timothy wasn't coming. I...I mustn't..."

Ignoring Miss Beakman's stuttering, and pretending not to notice that the poor girl looked scared out of her wits, Lord Brynne turned towards Tim. "I say, my dear fellow, I didn't think you were coming!" he shouted, as Tim approached the dock. "Sleeping like a babe when I left the house!"

"Should have woke me up, Syd! You ought to know I'd forgo a little sleep to sail on such a fair day."

"Well, you can't come in this boat. Too small for more than three, you know."

There was a pause here, while Lord Brynne thoughtfully rubbed his chin and appeared to be considering the alternatives. Charity had been looking determinedly at the boat bottom, her hands still clutching the sides in a grip that turned her knuckles white. Possibly because she felt Tim's eyes on her, she glanced up briefly through her lashes and instantly turned bright red. Tim was flushed, too, and not just from the exercise he'd had. Angela was considerably shaken by the look of yearning which passed between them. To think they wanted each other *that* much, yet still required outside interference to bring them together!

"There's only one thing to do," stated Lord Brynne at last. "We'll take two boats. The wind is too mild for the sloop, and we can row the dinghies if we must. Here, Tim," he ordered, moving aside so Tim could step forward. "You go with Miss Beakman and I'll take Miss Fairfax with me. Hand me one of the baskets, though. I've no notion of going without my lunch today! Careful, now! If Miss Beakman is sitting at the end, you must sit in the middle to keep the thing trimmed properly. Don't want to capsize, do you?"

Presently the deed was done. They'd ruthlessly bullied Charity into a position which was undoubtedly the most uncomfortable she'd ever endured, with, perhaps, the possible exception of the boat-house. They'd shamelessly lied, finagled and play-acted to get her exactly where they wanted her. Angela's only consolation was that they were doing it all for Charity's good. If Tim could not contrive to pull the truth out of her, certainly no one could. And once things were settled concerning Harry, Tim could explain his own feelings to Charity, and all would be well in the end. Watching them drift away from the dock, the sail billowing gently in the breeze and Tim's oars guiding them, Angela prayed it would be so.

"Are you thinking what I'm thinking, Miss Fairfax?" asked Lord Brynne, standing at her elbow.

She was startled to discover him so close to her and she felt flutterings in her stomach. It suddenly occurred to her that now *they* would be alone together in the other boat. She strove to keep her voice calm as she replied, "You are wondering if we have done the right thing?"

He nodded soberly.

"Yes, so am I." She wasn't referring only to Tim and Charity, for her growing attraction to Lord Brynne was becoming a rather disturbing part of each waking hour.

"Well, we've done it!" stated Lord Brynne. "And I'm of the philosophy that once you've done your best and your all, you must simply go on. It's a beautiful day, Miss Fairfax, and I would like nothing more than to take you out in my boat and show you Lake Derwentwater from the best possible vantage point—the middle of it! Surrounded by England's loftiest mountains, it is rather a, er, *spiritual* experience."

Angela caught the wicked gleam in his lordship's blue eyes. "You are teasing me again," she accused him, smiling. "I suppose you are referring to my penchant for stalking ghosts. I begin to think you made up those stories simply to plague me!"

"How can you say such a thing, Miss Fairfax?" he demurred, as he helped her into the other boat. "Besides, I wasn't referring to the ghosts. I was paying tribute to your angelic countenance."

Angela did not deign to reply, hoping to squelch this sort of talk. After deceiving Charity into the boating expedition, she did not feel in the least like an angel. She settled herself on the seat at the bow of the small boat, facing the stern. Lord Brynne sat down on one of the several horizontal boards in the middle of the boat and was facing the bow. The servant unwound the mooring rope and handed it to Lord Brynne, then set them adrift with a firm push of his foot.

"The wind will be stronger farther out," he commented as he plied the oars through the water, going in the opposite direction from Tim and Charity.

Angela thought he must be terribly strong, the way he seemed to manoeuvre the boat effortlessly through the gently rippling waters. As he bent forward for each stroke of the oar, his head came very close to hers. His eyes were downcast or fixed on the passing scenery as he rowed, and she was at leisure to examine him quite thoroughly. He had astonishingly thick lashes, she decided, and a noble brow. His dark curly hair shone lustrously in the sunlight. It looked finely textured and silky. Her fingers fairly itched with the urge to thread through those shiny locks and discover if they felt as soft as they looked.

Then, suddenly, as he bent near, the thick lashes lifted and he looked straight at her. "A penny for your thoughts, Miss Fairfax."

Angela quickly looked away, her heart hammering. "I wasn't thinking of anything, really," she lied. She seemed to being lying a great deal lately!

Lord Brynne lifted the oars out of the water and stored them in the stern by the picnic basket. Now the boat was eased along by the breeze. "You had rather a pensive look," he continued, stretching one long slim leg crossways in front of her and tucking the other under his seat. Angela watched him move, the languid ease of his athletic body mesmerizing her. "I thought perhaps you were thinking about your father and my mother," he added, eyeing her keenly.

"Why did you think so?" she asked, her brain feeling a trifle fuddled.

"Their conduct the other night disturbed you. I wondered if you were fretting over it."

This comment brought Angela's thoughts sharply back to focus. "No, I'm not fretting at all," she told him truthfully. "Perhaps at first I did, but not anymore."

He raised a brow. "Ah! Then you've forgiven them."

Angela frowned thoughtfully. "I don't believe 'forgiven' is the correct word," she said firmly. "Indeed, it would be quite ridiculous of me to presume to forgive anybody, unless, of course, someone had done something wrong to me personally. Papa is, as you said, a grown man and must make his own decisions."

"For my part, I'm glad of their relationship. You may be surprised to know, Miss Fairfax, that your father is the first man my mother has allowed herself to smile at since my father died four years ago."

Angela forbore to mention that Lady Brynne had done considerably more than smile at her papa, but only said, "Then you think it is a love match?"

He nodded.

"Then why don't they marry?" she wondered aloud.

"My mother adored my father," explained Lord Brynne, a small reminiscent smile curving his lips. "It is sometimes difficult to marry again when you were so happy with your first companion. In this modern age, a marriage based on love is something rare and beautiful, which usually occurs only once in a lifetime. Possibly she considers it risky to try her luck again."

Watching the play of emotions pass over his features, Angela was convinced that he was not merely surmising what his mother might have been thinking, but was actually expressing his own deeply felt thoughts on the subject. For some reason, the idea that Lord Brynne considered his relationship with his late wife something that could only occur once in a lifetime made her feel inexpressibly sad.

To offset this confusing rush of melancholy, Angela stuck her chin out and said, "Well, I don't believe in once-in-a-lifetime, fairy-tale romances. If, as you say, your mama is in love with my papa, the only really practical thing they should do is marry, for heaven's sake! You don't really suppose your father would wish her to pine away over his memory, do you? In my way of thinking, if people can love so very deeply once, why can't they do it twice, pray?"

At the end of this little speech, Lord Brynne seemed incapable of speaking. He stared at Angela with rather a startled expression. Alarmed that she might have offended him, she said in a great rush, "Oh, do teach me some boating terms, Lord Brynne. And tell me about the sky and storms and all! You know, 'Red sky at night, sailors delight, Red sky in morning, sailors take warning,' or something like that. My education is sadly lacking in nautical matters!"

Lord Brynne seemed to have recovered from his momentary lapse and grinned crookedly. "I had not thought your education lacking in much of anything, Miss Fairfax."

Angela blushed, but was spared further teasing about her propensity for bookishness. Lord Brynne obligingly began to tutor her in nautical lore and did it most entertainingly.

"Though a modest boat, Miss Fairfax," he began, his eyes snapping with enjoyment, "the dinghy has all the parts—well, nearly all the parts—of a much larger vessel! Let us begin with the keel, shall we? And progress by sure stages to the mast and the mainsail."

Angela leant back in her seat, which had, by the by, been thoughtfully supplied with a cushion and a lap-rug, and listened to Lord Brynne's directory of nautical terms. By the end of his lesson, she could not truthfully say that she knew the difference between a boom and a jib, but she had learned an important lesson nonetheless. It was this: green girls dare not spend too much time in the company of charming rakes, or else they are very likely to fancy themselves in love!

And that was all it was, she told herself. What she was feeling for Lord Brynne was just a fanciful version of real love. And even if she did love him, he could not love her, not with the vision of his first wife so firmly etched in his memory. And even if he did wish to marry her, Angela told herself most forcefully, he was a rake and she could not share her husband with anybody.

Despite these sobering reflections, Angela was enjoying herself. She laughed with uninhibited delight at Lord Brynne's jokes and relished every magic moment on the water with a sort of joyous desperation. Waves lapped against the boat in a hypnotizing caress as they drifted across the sun-dappled, amethyst waters of the lake. They ate their lunch as the afternoon wore on; crisp wafers and roast duck, watercress and grapes, raspberries swimming in little crocks of clotted cream, and rich red wine. Everything was perfect: the food, the lake, the marquess, everything.

"Oh, dear."

Angela was stirred from her euphoric state by his lordship's words and his look of concern.

"What is it?" she asked, sitting up straight and replacing her empty goblet in the picnic basket.

"Have you ever heard this little rhyme, Miss Fairfax? 'When the loft hill the mist doth bear, Let the seaman then of storms beware'?"

"No, I haven't. Is the mist settling round the mountains, then? I haven't even noticed!" She looked about and found that the mountain vales were indeed gradually filling up with a fine mist. "Are we in for a storm?"

"At sea, probably, but not here. However, the mist in the vales creeps over the lake by and by. We'd best make for shore."

The sun had nearly completed its arc across the sky by the time they returned to the dock, and Angela thought it must have been close to four o'clock. A servant was waiting to relieve them of the picnic basket and to moor the boat to the dock. But the other boat was still missing, and Sir Timothy and Charity were nowhere to be seen.

"Vicar Beakman will be back soon, if he's not already," said Angela worriedly. "I don't wish to put Charity at odds with her papa!"

"Perhaps Miss Beakman has a great deal more to worry about than one stolen afternoon, Miss Fairfax," he reminded her. "Why don't you go back to the house with the servant? I'll have him send the carriage round so Miss Beakman can be driven home when she gets back. You must be very tired."

Angela wasn't tired, but she was becoming a little chilled. Wrapping her arms about her, she said, "I want to wait for Charity. I feel responsible for her. But I will take that laprug and use it as a shawl, if you don't mind."

Lord Brynne gave orders to the servant and sent him on his way to the Abbey, but took the laprug from him and folded it in a neat triangle before gently placing it about Angela's shoulders. Pulling the ends together in the front and fashioning a sort of makeshift tie, he said teasingly, "Sailor's knots come in handy now and then, too, Miss Fairfax. This is called a reef knot!"

Angela laughed and impetuously seized Lord Brynne's hands as they released the bulky ends of the laprug. To her utter surprise, he turned his palms upward and clasped her wrists, pulling her to him.

As if she had done it a hundred times instead of never before, Angela's eyes fluttered shut as she drifted easily into Lord Brynne's arms. The sensation of his lean, hard body against her soft, compliant curves made her feel as if warm honey flowed through her veins. Thick, sweet, languorous feelings weakened her limbs till she felt as though she would surely fall if he did not continue to hold her.

When his lips—those very *capable* lips—touched hers, she gasped as a jolt of sheer pleasure pulsed through her. Then, as Lord Brynne tenderly, thoroughly and very capably kissed her, Angela forgot how very unwise it was to love a rake.

CHAPTER EIGHT

SYDNEY HEARD the carriage approach as if from afar. The muted clip-clop of the horse's hooves had a dreamy quality, hanging on the perimeter of his consciousness like a half-forgotten memory. But soon the noise grew louder and more encroaching, till at last he was forced to bring himself to a complete realization of his surroundings.

He opened his eyes and found his lips firmly attached to Miss Fairfax's. This must account for his state of dreamlike confusion! And her body was pressed against his, the lush curves of her breasts inciting his heart to a thudding rhythm. One of her hands was tangled in the hair at the nape of his neck and the other was fervidly caressing his back.

And where were *his* hands, he wondered. Since his mind was being bombarded with sensations from various parts of his body, he had to concentrate very hard to force his brain to locate his arms. Then, following each arm to its natural conclusion, he discovered one hand curved round her neck and the other just on the point of cupping her buttock.

Horrified to find himself in such a compromising position, but gratified and stirred to find Miss Fairfax a more than willing participant, he quickly disentangled himself and held Miss Fairfax at arm's length. The picture of wanton disarray she presented when he had this enlarged view of her nearly shattered his resolve. Her bonnet was askew, her hair a tangle of golden curls, her eyes were drooping and dilated, and her lips were swollen with kisses and parted. He was convinced that if he withdrew his support, she would fall like a boneless heap to the ground. This conviction might have appealed to his masculine vanity if he hadn't been so chagrinned by his own weakened limbs.

He darted a look towards the lane and saw, just as he expected to, the cabriolet, pulled up and awaiting their pleasure. The servant handling the ribbons, and Simon on the back, were both determinedly staring straight ahead and pretending not to have noticed his lordship in the throes of a passionate embrace. Devil a bit! It would be all over the servants' hall that Lord Brynne did not confine his amorous exploits to experienced demi-reps and worldly wives! Now the half of the household that did not already believe it of him would think him Harry's father, too!

"Miss Fairfax," he said at last in a firm tone. "I shall send you back to the Abbey immediately. I'll wait for Miss Beakman and Sir Timothy. Do you understand?"

Miss Fairfax's dazed look gradually sharpened to one of dismayed comprehension. In a flutter of nervousness, she straightened her bonnet, shoved wayward curls behind her ears and tugged at her skirt where it had been hitched up on one side. Then, avoiding his eyes entirely, she turned and walked to the carriage. He escorted her, but did not touch her again until he handed her up to the seat. To his astonishment, even that brief contact set his blood to boiling again.

As he watched the carriage drive away, Sydney was acutely aware that Harry was far from the only complication in his life. In fact, Miss Fairfax presented the more complicated dilemma of the two. Harry belonged with his mother, but where did Miss Fairfax belong? Certainly not in that sacred place in his heart which rightfully belonged to Caroline. *Or did she?*

Kissing Miss Fairfax had unleashed a swirl of tender emotions and strong physical desires, the like of which Sydney hadn't felt since his wife's death. None of the other women with whom he'd dallied over the past two years had affected him in such a way. Recognizing this fact made him feel unfaithful to Caroline! He knew it was a silly notion, since he'd actually made love to the others and had only kissed and caressed Miss Fairfax, but what he had shared with her was more than physical, it was a blending of souls, a deeper, more meaningful joining. It was very much like . . . love.

Sydney dragged his fingers through his hair. It couldn't be love! The sort of feelings he had had for Caroline could only occur once in a lifetime . . . couldn't they? He deemed it almost a sacrilege to contemplate marriage with another woman. But when he imagined Miss Fairfax married to someone else, something inside him recoiled at the very thought!

Sydney shook his head and walked slowly back to the dock and looked out over the darkening waters. He had a great deal of thinking and soul-searching to do. Finally in the distance he saw the other boat approaching. He sighed, hoping that Tim and Miss Beakman, at least, had settled things happily between them.

NOW ANGELA KNEW exactly how it felt to be human and vulnerable to one's own desires. Sitting on the edge of her bed and abstractedly twirling a ringlet round her index finger, Angela was in perfect sympathy with her father and Lady Brynne, Tim and Charity, and every other mortal being who had succumbed to passion. Now that she knew how delicious it felt to be kissed and caressed by the man you love, she wondered that anyone attained the wedded state with her virginity intact.

For there was never any question that what she felt for Lord Brynne was love. She was perfectly sure that had any other young man of her acquaintance tried to kiss her as Lord Brynne had kissed her, it might have been interesting, even pleasant in some cases, but never so intoxicating that she quite lost herself to all reason! Why, if the carriage hadn't come round and interrupted them . . .

Angela stood up and paced the floor. She would have to leave the Abbey. Yes, she loved Lord Brynne, but he still loved his first wife and had no intention of remarrying. And even if they did marry, she would be heartbroken if ever he were unfaithful to her. She would not stay and find herself swept along by her own passions and making the greatest mistake of her life. Certainly she did not think Lord Brynne meant to take advantage of her, but if she encouraged him, he might not be able to restrain himself. She felt a trifle wicked for thinking it, but she felt considerable pleasure in knowing that Lord Brynne had been quite as shaken by their embrace as she.

Subduing the rush of heat which bubbled up inside her at the memory of that lakeside embrace, Angela left her room and walked down the hall towards her father's bedchamber. She was already dressed for dinner in a pale pink sarsenet gown. It lacked an hour till the bell would be rung, and she was quite sure of finding her papa at his dressing table. She was reluctant to disturb his ritual pomading and primping, but she felt it was urgent that she talk to him and convince him to cut short their visit.

''Miss Fairfax?''

Angela turned and saw Lawrence standing at the head of the stairs. ''What is it, Lawrence?''

''Lord Brynne wishes to see you in the library, miss.''

Angela's palms felt damp. ''Is...is he alone, Lawrence?''

Lawrence's left brow lifted slightly, but he remained carefully expressionless. ''Sir Timothy is with him.''

Angela felt a bit anxious about putting off her interview with her father, and she didn't feel quite ready to face the marquess. However, she ought to be safe

enough in his lordship's company if there were someone else in the room. Besides, to be summoned to the
library could mean only one thing: news about Harry.

Angela followed Lawrence downstairs and walked
through the library door, which he held open. For
once, the prospect of news about Harry could not
crowd out disturbing feelings concerning Lord
Brynne, as they used to do. Today, above all else,
every fibre of her being reached out to the dark, imposing silhouette etched against the white Adam fireplace. All in evening black, with a crisp white
neckcloth bringing out the hint of bronze on his cheek-
bones and the cerulean blue of his eyes, Lord Brynne
returned her agitated gaze with one which revealed an
equal portion of disquiet.

"Sit down, Miss Fairfax," he said in measured
tones, with no hint of the teasing playfulness she was
used to.

She sat down and noticed, for the first time, Sir
Timothy sitting in a leather wing-chair. There was an
air of cheerfulness about him which could not be
missed, even by one as distracted as herself.

"As you must have guessed, we've come to some
conclusions about Miss Beakman," began Lord
Brynne, his eyes flickering over her, then fixing on a
point across the room. "Perhaps Tim can best explain."

Now Tim beamed. "Indeed, I should love to, Syd!"
Tim leaned forward and prepared to impart his news,
which, Angela concluded, had to be good or else he

wouldn't have looked so very happy. "Charity is *not* Harry's mother!"

Angela felt a flood of relief, followed immediately by a sense of disappointment. She was quite pleased to know that Charity's reputation would remain unblemished, but at the same time was frustrated to discover they were no closer to knowing who Harry's mother really was.

"Would you like to explain, Sir Timothy, or shall I just wish you happy and be done with it?" Angela gently teased.

Tim's grin broadened. "You may certainly wish me happy! But I do not mind telling you the details. It's like this, Miss Fairfax. Something did happen at the boat-house that night, but I'm pleased to tell you that even in my drunken state I did not do Miss Beakman the slightest dishonour. That is, of course, unless you consider a kiss a dishonour."

"Oh, no!" Angela quickly assured him, carefully avoiding looking at Lord Brynne. "If both partners are willing, I do not consider kissing dishonourable in the least!"

"You are tolerant of us mere mortals, are you not, Miss Fairfax?" he said, laughing. "No doubt angels like yourself are spared the temptations of the flesh!"

"Do go on, Sir Timothy!" urged Angela, thrown into a flutter of embarrassment. "Besides the kiss, did something else happen in the boat-house?"

"I asked her to marry me, Miss Fairfax! Can you credit it? I asked her to be my wife that night in the boat-house and promptly forgot all about it the next day! And she's forgiven me!''

Angela's eyes widened. "Then she went to Portsmouth because..."

"Because she could not bear to look at me, she said," admitted Tim. "She was very hurt, but also very angry with me. She kept waiting for me to come and declare myself to her papa, and when I did not, she thought I'd jilted her. She thought I was toying with her affections only so that she would allow me to kiss her! I stayed away because the vicar had forbidden me to come near her after he'd found out I'd kissed her, then she went away to Portsmouth. And all along she did not know I'd lost my memory of that night at the boat-house, but thought I'd purposely hurt and humiliated her. I wonder that she didn't grow to hate me! Oh, if only I'd had the courage to ask her to marry me when I was sober!''

"She did not tell her father of your proposal?'

"No. And her arrival at the vicarage on the day of Harry's appearance on the Abbey steps was pure coincidence. We have been going hey-go-mad with conjectures, haven't we? I can't tell you how relieved I am!''

Angela wrinkled her brow. "The only thing which still confuses me, Tim, is why she acted so oddly when I tried to discuss Harry with her. The subject seemed to distress her more than it ought.''

"Do you think so?" said Tim, clearly unimpressed. "Well, it must be attributed to the fact that

Charity is not used to discussing such indelicate subjects.''

"I must agree with Miss Fairfax," Lord Brynne interjected. "I wonder if Miss Beakman does know something about Harry, but is unwilling to tell us.''

"Well, as I told you before, Syd, I did not mention Harry to her today. I managed to get the truth out of her about the boat-house without revealing our suspicions about her in connection with Harry—thank God! And now nobody need know that we ever considered such a hideous possibility, except, of course, for Mr. Holmes. You don't think he'll bruit it about, do you?''

"No, I don't," was Lord Brynne's flat reply. "I would never have taken him into my confidence if I didn't trust him completely. Do you think you can speak to Miss Beakman about Harry, Tim? Seems you're the fellow who's most likely to get the facts out of her.''

"You make it sound as if she's hiding something, Syd," objected Tim. "And I don't think I like that above half! Besides, I don't think there are any facts to get out of her!''

"Don't put yourself in a pucker. I'm not implying that Miss Beakman is doing something wrong. I'm only wondering if she knows something, but is too timid to speak up.''

Angela forced herself to look at and speak directly to Lord Brynne, telling herself her emotions must not make her forget her concern for Harry. "Do you have another idea about who the mother or the father might be, my lord?'' She knew she had her own thoughts on the subject. She had not forgotten Granny Meg's admonition that they should ''look to the vicarage,'' though perhaps Lord Brynne had decided to discount the old woman's words along with the other particulars which had led them to suspect Miss Beakman.

''We were dead wrong about Miss Beakman,'' the marquess replied evasively. ''I wouldn't dare to say, even if I had a suspicion. When I have solid proof, then I shall tell you what I think. No more conjecturing for me, thank you!''

Angela had to respect his lordship's reticence, though it frustrated her. It was distressing how far they'd progressed in their mistaken idea about Charity Beakman. She turned to Tim and asked, ''Did you return Charity to the vicarage without incurring the wrath of her protective papa?''

''Got her home before he arrived. Going to be a tricky business telling that puffed-up prig of a parson that he's got me to look forward to as a son-in-law!''

''He doesn't really know you, Tim,'' said Lord Brynne. ''I'm sure he'll grow to like you tolerably well as time goes by.''

''Trouble is, will I ever grow to like *him?*'' Tim grumbled.

''That, my dear fellow, is the real question,'' said Lord Brynne, smiling for the first time since Angela had entered the room. Then he turned and caught her eye and the smile slid off his face like melting butter.

How very distressing, thought Angela, to have such a dampening effect on Lord Brynne's spirits! But it could only mean one thing: he must be hating himself for breaking his rake's code of honour and kissing her! And he was probably wondering, too, if he were to be obliged to defend himself to Lord Amesbury or be pressured into marrying her. It was to be hoped the opinion she'd expressed about kissing not being dishonourable between two willing participants might reassure him a little.

But the last thing she wanted was an apology from Lord Brynne for kissing her. Even if it meant nothing to him but a physical diversion, it had been something quite special to her. She did not want it belittled by an apology.

"Well, I've got to dress for dinner," announced Tim, standing up. "Dashed hungry! Suppose love does that to you, eh, Syd?"

Lord Brynne must have chosen to consider the question as purely rhetorical, because he did not reply, but moved to the window and stared out.

Angela stood up and hurried after Tim, but Lord Brynne detained her, saying, "Don't go, Miss Fairfax. I want to talk to you."

Now he will make his apology, she thought glumly. She sat down and watched dismally as he continued to stare out of the window. When Angela began to hope that she'd imagined his request for her to remain behind, he turned round. With his hands clasped behind his back, he walked slowly towards her, his blue eyes burning sapphire-bright as he looked at her.

From his expression, Angela couldn't tell if he wished to strangle her, beg her forgiveness or make love to her. Perhaps it was a little of all three. She wished it were the last... and she wished she *didn't* wish it were the last! Her breath caught in her throat and fear thrummed through her.

Just as he seemed about to speak, there was a scratch at the library door and Lawrence entered the room and announced Mr. Holmes. Angela wasn't sure if she was relieved or disappointed.

Lord Brynne sighed heavily and moved to stand by the mantelpiece as Mr. Holmes came in. "How do you do, Mr. Holmes?" he said wearily. "And what have you to report?"

Mr. Holmes removed his broad-brimmed hat, bowed respectfully to his lordship and Angela, mumbled his greetings, then stood mutilating his hat's brim with nervous fingers.

"I think we were wrong about Miss Beakman, my lord," he began.

"Indeed, we were, Mr. Holmes," Lord Brynne agreed. "Just this afternoon we came to that conclusion. What made you change *your* mind?"

"I believe I know who the mother is for certain, and it makes more sense, to my way of thinking."

"Who is it?" enquired Angela eagerly.

"Well, my lord, I took the liberty of asking Lawrence to fetch her...."

"To fetch her...? Surely, Mr. Holmes, you're not saying...?" Lord Brynne's eyebrows lowered forbiddingly.

"Did you want me, m'lord?"

All eyes turned to the door where Fran stood just upon the threshold. Her large blue eyes were wide and questioning and her freckles showed quite plainly on her pale face. She was obviously fearful, despite Lord Brynne's kind treatment of her in the past. But what nursery maid wouldn't be intimidated by a summons to his lordship's library, especially when she was asked to appear without her charge?

"Come in, Fran, and sit down," invited Lord Brynne, his calm, quiet manner calculated to put her at her ease. She came in and sat down on the sofa, her hands twitching at her apron hem. Lawrence shut the door and left them alone.

Lord Brynne moved to stand in front of her and in a gentle voice, demanded, "Franny, I want you to tell me everything you know about Harry."

"Wh-what do you mean, m'lord?" she stammered, her eyes grown as large as dishes.

"Mr. Holmes seems to think you have some sort of, er, connection with Harry you haven't told us about."

Fran threw Mr. Holmes a startled look, then covered her face with her hands and burst into tears.

"Calm yourself, child," whispered Angela, sitting down beside her on the sofa and stroking her hair. "We're your friends and we only want to help you. You can tell us anything, you know."

"I don't have anything to tell you!" said Fran between hiccupping sobs.

"Franny, there's no use in trying to hide it any longer," implored Mr. Holmes, moving closer to the sofa and looking quite miserable.

Fran reared up her head and wailed, "I thought you was my friend, Ned Holmes! I thought you was hangin' round me 'cause you liked me! Now I know differ'nt!"

"I heard you talking to Harry, Fran," Mr. Holmes went on, trying not to look hurt by Fran's accusations. "I heard you telling him how much you missed him when you went away and all. He's taken to you, Franny, in such a short time. It's as if he knew you before. And you always know just what to do to quiet him. Just as a mother would!"

"Well, you're wrong!" Fran burst out feelingly, lifting her red, swollen face from Angela's shoulder. "Harry's not my son. He's my brother!" Then she broke down in another violent torrent of tears.

To say that Angela was stunned by this revelation was rather inadequate. This was a twist in events she had not expected even in her wildest conjectures. Lord Brynne said nothing, but handed his handkerchief to Angela for Fran's use and looked very concerned.

After a few moments of wrenching sobs, Fran calmed herself at last and was eventually coaxed into taking a sip of watered wine. Presently she sat back against the sofa cushions and sighed. "I've been wantin' to tell you, but I dared not! I wanted you to keep Harry so's I could be near 'im!"

"Where's your mother?" Angela gently asked her.

"Dead" was the girl's sober reply. "That's why I brung Harry here. After Mum died, there was no one left to take care of 'im. Or, at least, no one what would!"

"What about your father?" enquired the marquess.

"*My* father's dead, but my father ain't Harry's father!" said Fran.

"Ah, yes," agreed the marquess. "Your note said he was born on the wrong side of the blanket."

"Yes, m'lord," Fran continued. "My mum's been a widow these past few years and feelin' poorly, too. She had a cottage in Keswick and I helped her with food an' all with the money I made workin' at th' Abbey. She had a job at the foundling home, cookin', but she was sick with a cough part o' th' time and bedridden. When she started breedin'..." The girl paused, clearly embarrassed. "Well, she said we was to keep the baby a secret between us. She said she daren't tell even the babe's father. Then before she started increasin' too much, she went away to m'brother's in Middleton and had the baby there. After a time, he told her to leave 'cause he said the baby was a bastard and he wouldn't raise a bastard, even if'n it was his half-brother! Then my mum died. It's my opinion she died of a broken heart!"

This speech brought forth a fresh flow of tears, but Fran tried hard to suppress them.

"Your mother was certainly clever in hiding her pregnancy from the local people. And the fact that she gave birth to the child as far away as Middleton must account for their continued ignorance after the babe was born," mused Lord Brynne, rubbing his chin thoughtfully. "How did you ever contrive to bring Harry here, Fran?"

"Sunday last, Mrs. Hobbs gave me the afternoon off to visit my mum. Mrs. Hobbs knew Mum was sickly. I hitched a ride to Middleton, but when I got there Mum was already gone and buried, and my brother was fixin' to throw little Harry on the parish! I told 'im I'd take Harry and care for 'im, not thinkin' how I could do it. My brother drove me to the woods t'other side of Keswick, and I walked th' rest o' the way. By then I'd decided what I was goin' to do, so I dared not hitch a ride, or walk down the main road 'cause someone might recognize me. You know the rest, m'lord!"

"What about your other brothers and sister, Fran? I thought you came from a large family."

Fran flushed and bit her lip. "I lied about that, m'lord. My brother and I, and Harry o' course, are the only children. All the maids wanted to take care of Harry, so's I made up all that about bein' from a large family. I knew he'd want me over t'others."

Lord Brynne sighed. "Well then, Fran, now tell us who the father is."

"I don't know, m'lord!" sobbed Fran. "Mum wouldn't tell me. She was that ashamed! She said she feared 'im 'cause just before she left for Middleton he come to the cottage, saw how she was increasin' and threw a rare humdurgeon fit! Said if it ever got about that she was breedin' with his babe, he'd lose his position. He told her never to come back to the valley. I didn't know what to do, m'lord! I could only think of bringin' Harry to Castlerigg Abbey, where I've been treated so fairly m'self! Please don't be angry!"

"I'm not angry with you, Fran," the marquess replied soothingly. "You did what you thought best at the time. But how I'd relish strangling the irresponsible rogue who left your mother in such dire straits!"

Lord Brynne paced the floor and dragged his hands through his hair till it stood on end. Except for the soft thud of the marquess's slippers against the carpet as he strode the room's length, back and forth, all was quiet. Mr. Holmes seemed deep in thought and Angela imagined that Fran was too spent to feel much of anything at this point, except perhaps a lightened burden in having shared her hard-kept secret. For her part, Angela was grateful to have at least a portion of the mystery solved.

The late afternoon sun was fading and a chambermaid crept into the dim room to light the candles and stoke up the dying fire. After the chambermaid left, the marquess suddenly turned on his heel and said, "You'd best return to Harry, Fran. And for God's sake, don't worry any more. Something will be arranged so that you and Harry needn't be separated. As for Harry's father, he shall be dealt with."

Fran thanked Lord Brynne in a quavery voice and cast him a look of complete trust before she left the room.

Lord Brynne turned to Mr. Holmes and said, "You've done well, Mr. Holmes."

"I've my suspicions about who the father might be, m'lord," he said after a pause.

"As do I," replied his master with a keen, quick look and a nod of his head. "And I'm persuaded we think alike on the subject. Don't trouble yourself about him. I want to collect a little proof before I confront the fellow.''

"Yes, of course, my lord," said Mr. Holmes, his expression never changing. "If you won't be needing me any more...?''

"Yes, you may go. Thank you again. Good day, Mr. Holmes." Lord Brynne followed Mr. Holmes to the door, shook his hand and closed the door behind him.

Once again Angela was alone with Lord Brynne. Standing up, she moved to the fireplace and with her back to him, pretended to be toasting her hands. In truth she had no need of a warming fire. Lord Brynne's mere presence in the room was enough to keep her quite glowing with heat. But she needed a moment to compose herself and collect her thoughts before confronting him. She prayed he would keep his distance, or else her brain would become hopelessly befuddled.

Soon she became unnerved by his continued silence and she turned round to face him. He stood leaning against the back of the sofa, watching her intently.

"Lord Brynne," she began hurriedly, afraid he would begin his apology before she had a chance to speak. "What an afternoon we have had!" Then, realizing that he might think she referred to the kiss on the dock and not the revelation of who Harry's mother was, Angela felt confusion and alarm flow through her. "I mean about Fran's mother being Harry's mother, you know! We thought all would be solved when we knew who his mother was, but—alas!—that simply is not the case, is it?"

"Miss Fairfax, why don't we set aside that question for now? I wish to—"

"But how can we, Lord Brynne?" interrupted Angela, gulping down the hurtful fullness in her throat and pressing on determinedly. "After all, we are so near to solving the entire mystery. You have indicated to Mr. Holmes that you have strong suspicions of who the father might be, and feel quite certain he shares your ideas. I understand that you do not wish to disclose your thoughts on this subject, but perhaps it would not be amiss if I confided my own suspicions to you?"

"Dash it all, Miss Fairfax—Angela! I don't want to talk about Harry! We can talk about Harry later, but we may not have another opportunity to be alone for some time and I wish to tell you something!" Lord Brynne moved from behind the sofa and walked purposely towards her, the determined expression on his face and the glitter of his blue eyes nearly melting Angela's resolve.

When he stood before her, she stepped back as close to the fire as she dared. "I begin to think you do not wish me ever to know who Harry's father is!" she accused him impetuously, lifting her chin and staring defiantly into his eyes. "Scruples about my delicate sensibilities as a pure maiden hold you back, I suppose! You are concerned that my innocence and naïveté about the world will make me ill prepared for the blow of knowing who Harry's father really is! Well, it's too late to be thinking about all that, don't you think?"

Lord Brynne raised his brows. "Miss Fairfax, that it would be a blow to you is doubtful, and as to your, er, delicate sensibilities, why I—"

"We both know who Harry's father is, Lord Brynne!" Angela blurted out, all the agitation and tumbled emotions of the past few days culminating and urging her to speak bluntly. "Granny Meg said we should look to the vicarage. We did, but we were looking at the wrong person. We were misled by Charity's coincidental return to the neighbourhood on the same day that Harry appeared on the Abbey's doorstep. Fran said her mother worked in the kitchen at the foundling home until she became too ill. I happen to know that Vicar Beakman visits the foundling home at least once a week! These facts, added to Charity's agitation whenever we speak of Harry makes me think 'tis the vicar, my lord! The vicar is Harry's father!"

Lord Brynne's eyes widened, then narrowed. "All this merely constitutes circumstantial evidence, Miss Fairfax. And you know how unsatisfactory circumstantial evidence is when building a case against someone. There must be something else which makes you suppose the vicar is Harry's father." He stepped closer and leaned slightly forward. His look was very penetrating. "Pray, what has the vicar done to make you suspect him of trifling with women?"

"Well, it's the way he..." Angela stopped, suddenly embarrassed. How could she explain the way the vicar looked at her? But this matter was too important to let embarrassment stand in her way. "He looks at me in such a way... It's as if... as if I'd forgotten to put my clothes on! I don't know how to explain it any better!"

Lord Brynne eyes flashed blue fire. "I noticed he had an instant liking for you, but could not see the expression in his eyes as he looked at you. It's as bad as that, is it? He hasn't touched you, has he?"

Angela could not mistake the protective undercurrent in Lord Brynne's question. Her eyes searched his, striving to understand the feelings behind the murderous glint she saw reflected there.

"N-no, not in the manner I suppose you mean," she replied shyly. Certainly not in the manner Lord Brynne had touched her! Her cheeks flamed at the memory.

"I can guess your thoughts at this moment!" He sighed heavily and reached for her hand. She trembled as he pressed her fingers in a warm clasp. "Forgive me, Miss Fairfax! It must seem hypocritical of me to be enraged by the way the vicar looks at you when I myself..." His voice trailed off.

"Oh, please don't apologize," cried Angela, snatching her hand away. "You'll spoil everything if you do!" She turned away, biting her lip and wringing her hands with agitation. "If this is what you wish to talk to me about, pray do not. I'm well aware that our embrace on the dock meant nothing to you, my Lord Brynne, except perhaps a little titillation, but it meant a great deal to me! And, never fear, I've no intention of trying to bring you up to scratch over a mere kiss or two. Now, if you don't mind, I must go and dress for dinner!''

Lord Brynne looked stunned. ''Don't go, Miss Fairfax! Let me explain! It's just that I was married before, as you know, and it is difficult to—''

''Yes, I know,'' Angela interrupted quietly. ''You've no intention to remarry. I pity you, my lord. What a strange idea you have of love, if you think it must needs cut you off from happiness for the rest of your life because you loved your first wife so well! I had always been wont to believe that the more you love, the more you are capable of loving. Your heart expands to accommodate whomever you wish to include in your affections.''

Then, striving to control her voice and emotions, Angela added, ''But it does not signify why you cannot marry me, because I have no intention of shackling myself for life to a man who cannot be faithful to me! Doubtless you think me sadly behind the times, but I cannot help it!'' Then, appalled by her outspokenness, Angela walked to the door. She dared not look at Lord Brynne. He probably thought her an utter noddy for refusing an offer of marriage he hadn't even extended!

''My lord,'' announced Lawrence, suddenly appearing at the door just as Angela was about to exit. ''Vicar Beakman!''

Then the vicar burst into the room and demanded, ''What is this business I hear about my Charity and that drunken libertine, Sir Timothy Clives?''

CHAPTER NINE

"VICAR BEAKMAN, you come at a highly inopportune time!" said the marquess, abandoning his usual tactful handling of the man. "I'm having an important conversation with Miss Fairfax!"

Though she had been desperate to flee just a moment before, Angela now felt bound by loyalty to Harry to stand her ground. How dared Vicar Beakman act so high and mighty when he had committed such a moral crime, the likes of which any Christian would deplore? "Lord Brynne," she began, turning resolutely to face the marquess. "Don't you think this is the perfect time for you to question Vicar Beakman about that little matter we were discussing?"

"What *are* you talking about?" the vicar demanded irritably.

Lord Brynne moved swiftly to stand between Angela and the door, as if he might bodily block her if she tried to escape again. Then, ignoring the vicar, he addressed Angela. "I don't agree with your suspicions, Miss Fairfax," he stated flatly. "And I'm not done with talking to you! Do you think you can say such things to me, then walk out the door?"

"What suspicions?" enquired the vicar, exasperated. "I came to talk to you about Charity and Sir Timothy!"

"That will have to wait, Beakman!" the marquess informed him, glowering at Angela. "I have some private words to say to Miss Fairfax which I wish to say *now*! And I should be best pleased if you'd wait in the drawing-room, Vicar!"

Angela put her hands on her hips. "Nothing you have to say to me, Lord Brynne, can be as important as finding Harry's father!"

"What I have to say to you includes information about Harry's father, Miss Fairfax. I warn you, say no more!" he finished sternly.

"You've found Harry's father?" said the vicar, struggling to understand the turbulent scene being played out before him.

Angela jerked her head and glared at the vicar. "How can you affect such innocence, Vicar Beakman? We all know that *you* are Harry's father!"

Lord Brynne groaned and slapped a hand over his eyes. Vicar Beakman's reaction was slightly different; he fainted. Luckily Lord Brynne removed his hand just in time to notice the vicar's rolling eyes and crumbling posture. He caught the huge clergyman before he could gash his head on a nearby table, then dragged him to a wing-chair and propped him up in it.

"Don't just stand there, Miss Fairfax!" barked the marquess. "Fetch some brandy! There, on the table! And some sal volatile, if you have some in your reticule. Be quick!"

Angela scurried to do his bidding, dismayed to see the vicar looking so white and lifeless. She handed the glass of brandy to Lord Brynne, saying, "Goodness, I did not think he would be so faint-hearted. One would almost suppose he isn't guilty!"

"He's not guilty!" said the marquess shortly, pressing the glass against the vicar's slack lips. "And if you had let me explain, we might have avoided this monumental *faux pas!*"

Brandy dribbled off the vicar's chin, but a few drops had found their way down his throat and he moaned weakly.

"You could have explained earlier, instead of offering me that horrid apology!" Angela retorted, placing the opened bottle of sal volatile beneath the vicar's proboscis. The vicar's eyes fluttered briefly and his head lolled from side to side against the back of the chair.

"I had every intention of telling you, but I did not think it expedient to tell you immediately," returned the marquess in a hissing whisper. "I did not suppose that you meant to accuse the vicar the moment you clapped eyes upon him! Besides, there has been something else more pressing on my mind this afternoon which I wanted to discuss with you first. No, not the apology, though I did mean it quite sincerely when I said I was sorry I compromised you! But not for the reasons you mentioned, Miss Fairfax! If you'd only given me a moment's leisure to explain.... Oh, but never mind! I can't speak freely in front of *him!*" He glared at the vicar in frustration.

"The vicar is still unconscious," said Angela, replacing the lid on the bottle of pungent restorative and setting it down on a nearby table. "You're quite right that we oughtn't to continue our quarrel in front of the vicar, but you can at least tell me who you think Harry's father is!"

Lord Brynne sighed, but probably felt it useless at this point to keep silent. "It all began to make sense to me when it was revealed that Fran's mother was Harry's mother. Joseph drives the vicar everywhere, including to the foundling home in Keswick each week. I considered the vicar, as you did, but quickly dismissed him as a possibility when I remembered certain facts. For example, when the vicar came to see us yesterday, Joseph wasn't with him. I wondered about that, since Joseph has ever been a most reliable companion to the vicar, taking great pride in driving him about the countryside. I supposed Joseph to be in the stable, socializing with the stable-hands, though he does not usually do so. But I've a notion Joseph wasn't with the vicar at all that day! And you may recall that when the note was tucked into the squabs of the carriage at the George, the vicar was paying calls with Miss Beakman. He couldn't have delivered the note. He couldn't be in two places at once! But where was Joseph, pray tell?"

Angela's eyes widened. "And the person who left that note and the note left in Harry's basket, would have to be very quick on his feet! The vicar is too large to run very fast, but Joseph looks quite athletic, despite his height!"

The vicar was groaning now and striving to focus his eyes. "Yes, and this could also account for Charity's reaction whenever Harry was spoken of," added the marquess hurriedly. "Perhaps she suspected Joseph of it, but was too frightened of him to speak. He's quite intimidating, you know! But we must remember that all this still hinges on that first clue from Granny Meg. I don't know whether we can truly depend on the accuracy of her words!"

"Well, I believe her," said Angela firmly. "But something else still puzzles me. Why would Joseph be so concerned with his reputation? It made sense to me that the vicar would wish above all things to guard his reputation, but why would Joseph feel the same urgency?"

"Do you suppose the good vicar would keep Joseph on if he knew he had seduced a local widow? Joseph did not want to lose his position!"

"Yes, it all makes sense. But so did our other theory! How can we be sure?"

"We have been overlooking someone who might help us exceedingly," replied Lord Brynne. "Someone who has actually seen the villain depositing his notes!"

"You mean...?" Angela's eyes lit with understanding.

The marquess nodded, then turned back to the vicar. "Beakman? Beakman, are you feeling more the thing?" He spoke rather loudly, and gently slapped the vicar's heavy jowl.

"What's the matter? Where am I . . . ?" The vicar's dazed look gradually sharpened and he stared at Angela. "Ye Gods, now I remember! Young lady, you have greatly disappointed me! How dare you suggest that I . . . that *I* am Harry's father?"

"Never mind that now," broke in Lord Brynne. "Did Joseph come with you today, Vicar?"

The vicar looked confused. "Yes, of course he did. Always does unless he's too sick to sit up."

"Was he too sick to accompany you the day before yesterday when you and Charity came to the Abbey?"

The vicar's brows furrowed. "Believe he was! Got over it quickly, though. But what has that to do with anything? I came here to talk about that young jackanapes, Clives, not about the constitution of my servant!"

The marquess straightened up from leaning over the vicar and moved to ring the bell-pull hanging near the fireplace. Lawrence must have been just outside the door, because he instantly appeared. "Fetch Zeus, Lawrence," instructed the marquess. "I believe he may be in the nursery with Fran and Harry!"

Lawrence quickly withdrew and returned moments later with Zeus. The dog bounded forward to greet his master, wagged his tail at Angela, then noticed the vicar. He immediately sniffed the vicar's trouser legs, but showed no particular interest or animosity towards the still dazed clergyman.

"Come, Zeus," said his master. "We're going outside to see an old friend. Come, boy!"

"What are you doing, my lord?" the vicar called after him, but Lord Brynne ignored the question and strode with his dog out of the room, down the hall and towards the front door. Angela followed closely behind, her heart pounding with nervous excitement.

When they emerged into the early twilight, they looked about and discovered the vicar's carriage sitting in quite the far corner of the courtyard, a shadowy form hunched over in the front seat. As they approached the carriage, Joseph's mouth gaped open and he eyed Zeus with horror. It was soon apparent why Joseph was less than delighted by the sight of his lordship's amiable dog, for Zeus did not cherish amiable feelings for the vicar's servant.

Zeus growled and lunged towards the carriage. Joseph dropped the horses' ribbons and shrank back against the carriage seat, pulling up his long legs and hugging them against his chest. By then Zeus was barking furiously and lathering at the mouth.

"Call that blasted cur off, or I'll kick his teeth in!" snarled Joseph.

"Not until you tell me why Zeus has taken such a sudden and strong dislike to you," replied the marquess in an even, unperturbed manner which must have further infuriated Joseph.

"He's never liked me!" insisted Joseph, his eyes bulging as Zeus came closer and closer to the carriage. Zeus could easily jump up onto the carriage seat and probably was only kept from doing so by his master's continued calm manner.

"To my recollection, Zeus has never disliked any-body. But I imagine that he would object strenuously if someone should seem threatening to me, or seem a threat to the Abbey and its inhabitants. Pray tell, Joseph, is it possible that you constitute a threat to someone at the Abbey?"

"Begging your pardon, my lord, but that's plain nonsense!" screeched Joseph, kicking at the carriage sides as Zeus leapt and snapped his huge teeth in the air. The jarring of the carriage and the deafening barks of the dog were making the horses nervous. They pranced and threw back their black-maned heads in mounting agitation.

"I grow impatient, Joseph," said the marquess, an underlying thread of steel beneath his calm words. "If I must raise my voice to get my point across, I fear Zeus may interpret my change of tone as permission to attack. Did you write the notes, Joseph? Are *you* Harry's father?"

Joseph did not reply, but darted his eyes about as if seeking escape. Then, seeming to make a sudden and desperate decision, he seized the carriage ribbons and flipped them smartly against the horses' backs. The horses immediately reared up and lunged forward, jerking the front carriage wheels off the ground and breaking into a gallop.

Angela gasped and stepped back, aware that the horses might be a bit clumsy in their frightened state and she did not wish to be trampled. Stumbling a little, she was grateful when Lord Brynne slipped a steadying arm about her waist.

"Yes, I wrote the notes!" yelled Joseph as he drove away. "I'm the little bastard's father. And you can tell the vicar that I'll see 'im in Hell!"

"Goodness, what a horrid man!" exclaimed Angela, coughing in the cloud of dust created by the departing carriage.

"And a thief, too," said Lord Brynne, grimly watching the carriage disappear through the lodge gates and into the gathering mist which crept up from the lake. "What a fool! Now he'll have the law after him!"

"Shall we stop 'im, my lord?" shouted one of the stable-lads. A group of servants had gathered in the courtyard, attracted by the commotion and more than willing to take part in an exciting chase.

"No. I don't want any of you putting yourselves in danger. Joseph seems a foolish and, therefore, possibly a dangerous man. One of you may take word to the constable, if the vicar agrees to it. Is he still in the library?"

"Indeed not, m'lord!" came Lawrence's voice from the Abbey steps. "The vicar was watching from here, m'lord. He heard and saw it all, and he's fainted dead away!"

A light shone forth from the opened front door of the Abbey. Peering through the grey light of dusk, Angela saw Lawrence standing over a large, dark lump with outstretched arms and legs, which lay like a great animal-skin rug just inside the door.

"He certainly swoons easily," observed Angela.

"Yes, and I suppose I'd better go in and prepare myself to soothe the rector's outraged sensibilities, and listen to his moral homilies on the perfidy of the human race, when he comes to," Lord Brynne said wryly. "'Twill be a task of monumental proportions, I fear, and take half the night! We shall have to defer our talk till the morning, Miss Fairfax. But make no doubt, we *will* talk!"

Angela was suddenly aware that Lord Brynne's arm was still encircling her waist. Some of the servants were yet milling about, muttering and exclaiming over the recent excitement, and Angela noticed several curious looks directed towards the marquess and herself. They probably were busily speculating on how soon she would become, or whether or not she already was, another of Lord Brynne's conquests!

Grateful that the light concealed her blush of mortification, she pulled herself free and stepped back a little before looking up at the marquess. The breeze sifted through his dark hair and his eyes looked very bright and luminous. She swallowed nervously and forced herself to speak. "I should be more than willing, and certainly grateful, to be included in a discussion about Harry's future, now that we know the particulars of his past, my lord," Angela carefully recited. "But as to any other subject of conversation . . . I do wish you would forgive anything I said to you earlier and consider it merely the ravings of a woman half mad with worry—over Harry, you know! I did not intend to offend you!"

When Lord Brynne did not reply, but continued to look at her, a smile tugging at one corner of his beautifully sensual, extremely capable mouth, Angela's courage faded away with the last pale rays of the sun. She turned and ran into the house, past the prostrate vicar and gawking servants and up to her room.

MUCH, MUCH LATER that evening, Sydney wearily climbed the stairs to his bedchamber. What a day it had been! Once the vicar had been restored to his senses, Sydney had been obliged to listen patiently as he railed on about Joseph's traitorous behaviour and moral decrepitude, dwelling eloquently and at length on the servant's powers of deception.

"Indeed, my lord," the vicar had confided in tones of strong resentment, "I was never so deceived in my life! I thought Joseph the very model of propriety. I am deeply pained that someone I trusted so completely could have played me so foul a trick! Prime cattle they were—my beautiful black horses! And my carriage, so well sprung, so well suited in style and colour to a man of my profession! Where shall I ever find the blunt for just such another rig?"

It was apparent after an hour of this sort of talk that the vicar was more shocked and dismayed by Joseph's thievery than by his selfish seduction and abandonment of Harry's mother. Sydney could understand the vicar's attachment to his cattle and carriage, but he could not feel that Joseph's thievery was the more reprehensible of the two crimes. To stubble the vicar's tirade of complaints of ill-use at the hand of his trusted servant, Sydney introduced the subject of Tim and Charity.

This brought on another rush of self-pity, with the vicar brought nearly to the point of tears as he deplored the conduct of his thankless daughter. Sydney was close to the end of his tether where the vicar was concerned, but a strong sense of friendship for Tim helped him endure another hour's worth of Beakman's self-indulgent conversation. At the end of the hour, he had convinced the vicar that Tim was no longer the drinking man he used to be. He poured more balm on the vicar's paternal wounds with the hint that Tim might even be prepared to present his future father-in-law with another rig if his own was not recovered.

Finally, enveloped in Sydney's best cashmere lap-rug, his feet set upon a hot brick, and with his belly full of Sydney's best port, the vicar was driven away to the vicarage in a state of great physical comfort and with a mind put much more at ease about the loss of his own means of transportation. But no sooner had Sydney sent the vicar on his way, when the constable turned up.

Quite famished by then, Sydney called for food to be sent up to the library and he sat down with the constable and discussed Joseph over turtle soup, ham, cauliflower and roast potatoes, with a fruity steamed pudding for dessert.

The constable was a simple, straightforward sort of man, and he did not waste his lordship's time with meaningless chatter, but simply informed him that

Joseph had been intercepted at the toll-gate south of Keswick and was safely behind bars. If Lord Brynne would be so kind as to drive into Keswick at his convenience, he would be needed to swear an affidavit concerning the theft of the vicar's rig. With a lenient judge, Joseph would probably not be sent to the gallows unless previous crimes should be discovered, implying that he was a hardened criminal.

During the constable's visit, Tim had popped his head into the library and assured Sydney that everyone was in possession of the facts and had readily excused him from dinner so that he might see to the details. Tim assured him that he would keep the others entertained with ghost stories of Windy Grange.

Yes, it had been a long, difficult day! And full of revelations! At last Sydney reached his bedchamber and glanced longingly down the hall towards the other wing where Angela's room was located. He knew they had all gone to bed long before. He let himself into the room and discovered his valet napping in a chair by the dressing-table. Sydney tapped him on the shoulder to wake him, and the valet helped him undress and remove his boots, stoked up the fire and left Sydney to himself.

Easing himself beneath the warm quilts and counterpane, he sought slumber in vain. Well, if he could not sleep, he would think about Miss Angela Fairfax. It was a pleasant occupation, but not especially conducive to repose. Her angelic, stubborn little face seemed constantly before him. And the way she felt in his arms, and her impetuous confession that their embrace had meant something special to her, were harder still to forget.

It had not taken Sydney long that afternoon to decide that he was in love with her. But it had taken another hour's reflection in the quiet and solitude of his library to decide what to do about it. Then, suddenly, it became quite clear: he would marry her if she'd have him. Everything she'd said about a person's capacity to love being limited only by that person's willingness to love made a great deal of sense to him. And more than that, his heart would not be denied. He was quite sure that if he let Miss Fairfax slip away and out of his life, his heart would sustain another wound similar to the one inflicted when Caroline died.

As for Caroline... Sitting up, Sydney reached for the miniature portrait of his wife which he kept on a table by the bed. He traced with affection her strong, lively features and smiling eyes. Caroline had been a loving woman, the warmth of her affections encompassing a great number of people. She would not wish him to deny himself the strongest and most fulfilling kind of love—the love between a man and a woman, a husband and wife. For from such a love came the extension of family and all the delights attached to children.

Yes, Sydney's heart felt quite large enough to love Angela and the children who would come, God willing, as a result of their union, and to keep his love for Caroline as a warm memory, locked away in that part of his heart which belonged to the past. His future belonged to Angela now, and Wellesley.

He harboured no fears that his son and Angela might not rub along well together. Wellesley would undoubtedly adore Angela. And he was quite sure that if Angela could take the plight of an abandoned infant so much to heart, she could not help but take an affectionate interest in Wellesley, too. He opened the drawer of his bedside table and put the portrait away.

Then Sydney grimaced as he remembered the other things Angela had said that afternoon. She seemed convinced that his rakish behaviour would continue even after he married. She would have to be made to believe otherwise, or she would never agree to their betrothal.

Suddenly Sydney's musings were interrupted by a knock at the door. "Good God," he muttered to himself as he got up out of bed. "What now?"

He opened the door just a crack and discovered his diminutive mother smiling up at him. By the light of the candle she held, he could see she was still fully dressed.

"Mama!" he exclaimed, opening wide the door and admitting her into the room. "What are you doing up? Nothing's amiss, is it?"

"No, nothing at all, silly boy," his mother assured him, walking briskly to a settee by the fire and sitting down, tucking her small, daintily clad feet beneath her. "Come sit down," she ordered cheerfully, patting the cushion next to her. "It has been an age since we've had a comfortable coze together, just you and I, and there's no better time than the present!''

Sydney raised a dubious brow. ''Indeed, I should think some other time a little more convenient, Mama. I've had a difficult day, you know. And, as you can see, I'm in my nightshirt and cap, ready to sleep!''

''Yes, dear, I can see that! You always looked so precious in your night toggery! But Percy and I feel this matter must be dealt with immediately, Sydney. Angela wants to leave Castlerigg Abbey!''

His attention captured completely, Sydney sat down next to his mother. ''Leave the Abbey? Why?'' But he knew why.

His mother clicked her tongue and shook her head. ''She won't say why, Sydney, only that now that it has been discovered who Harry's parents are, she wants to go home and prepare for the London Season next year. I thought she was enjoying herself here at the Abbey, but tonight she moped about like a lovesick schoolgirl! Even Tim's ghost tales of Windy Grange did not pull her out of the megrims! What have you done to her, Sydney?'' she demanded with a penetrating look.

''Well, I—''

But before he could complete his confession, Lady Brynne spoke again. ''Whatever you did, it was probably something of a compromising nature, and I assure you, Sydney, that I think it expedient that you marry the child!''

''As a matter of fact—''

"And not simply because you compromised her, dearest, but because I'm convinced that you love her!"

"I do—"

"And don't tell me you don't love her. I've seen the way you look at her. Don't try to deny it!"

"Mama, I wouldn't dare—"

"And please, none of that nonsense about being lucky to have already been blessed with one true love in your life. Caroline was a dear girl, but so is Angela! And Caroline would think you an absolute slowtop not to recognize it when life is offering you yet another chance for happiness. This will doubtless come as quite a shock to you, Sydney, but I, too, have found happiness with someone!"

"Is that so?" he said, feigning an appropriate modicum of surprise and suppressing a grin. "But who can have replaced my father in your heart?"

"Replaced is not the word which best describes my affection for Percy," said the dowager, beaming. "I loved your father dearly. I love Percy dearly. I share my heart with the two of them. I find I have quite enough affection to encompass them both. And so do you, Sydney!"

"Indeed, I shall *try* to love Lord Amesbury, if you wish it," he replied soberly.

"Impudent boy!" admonished the dowager, tapping him on the shoulder. "You know I meant Caroline and Angela!"

Sydney joined in her laughter and, squeezing her small chin between his thumb and forefinger, kissed her lightly on the nose.

Satisfied that she had made her point, Lady Brynne stood up. "Now I must retire. It's nearly midnight, I believe."

"Do you have a strict schedule to keep, Mama, when it comes to retiring?" Sydney innocently enquired.

The dowager tittered and fluttered her hands like a small bird. "Of course not, Sydney! But I must allow myself so many hours for my beauty sleep, you know!"

"Of course," Sydney replied with a sly wink.

"Have you something in your eye, Sydney?" she asked him beatifically.

"No, Mama. Oh, and I do thank you for your kind advice. You've quite convinced me to marry the girl!"

"You were always an intelligent child," approved the dowager, as she lifted her candle and turned to the door. "Good night, my love!"

"Good night, Mama!"

Sydney chuckled as he climbed back into bed. Two-and-thirty and still receiving visits and admonishings from his mama! But that would change once she was married to Lord Amesbury and he was married to Angela. Then he sobered, remembering Angela's fears that he would be unfaithful. Somehow he must convince her that he was worthy of her trust!

CHAPTER TEN

"LOR', MISS, I wish'd Harry'd take his foot out o' his mouth, so's you could see his new tooth," said Fran, leaning over Harry's crib and smiling fondly down at the child.

"How he does like to sharpen those new little pearls on his toes!" Angela laughed as she leaned over the opposite side of the crib. At the sound of Angela's laughter, Harry stopped the industrious chewing of his foot and smiled up at her, revealing the tiny white addition to his short row of teeth on the bottom. Angela felt a tender tug at her heart, which turned suddenly into a sharp pain of sadness. She wouldn't be here to see and appreciate Harry's next tooth; she would be long gone from Castlerigg Abbey and all its occupants.

Angela blinked away the start of tears. She dared not think of her departure and how much she would miss the Abbey, the beautiful Lake Country, and the people she'd come to like so well. And most of all, she dared not dwell on her separation from Lord Brynne and how it would surely make her miserable for the rest of her life. He had said they would talk today, but it was already past noon and she had not yet seen him about the Abbey. At breakfast she was told that he was closeted with Mr. Holmes in the library and that he had sent his apologies to be excused from dining with the guests.

"I wonder what his lordship will do with me and Harry," said Fran now, her eyes searching Angela's for reassurance. Angela felt she could readily give Fran the assurance she needed, for she had no doubt that the marquess would deal fairly and kindly with them.

"His lordship is a good master, and a very kind man, Fran," said Angela, reaching over to squeeze Fran's shoulder. "I'm quite certain you'll be pleased with the arrangements. He promised you that you wouldn't be separated."

"That he did, didn't he?" said Fran, beaming. "I'm so glad I brought Harry here. I did right, didn't I, miss?"

"Under the circumstances, I think it was the best thing you could have done," agreed Angela. But it had certainly initiated a closeness between her and the marquess which might not have developed without Harry's mystery to solve, thought Angela. If she had remained aloof, as she had tried to do at the outset of the visit, maybe she wouldn't have fallen head over ears in love with Lord Brynne.

"But you could have told me Harry was your brother and spared us a great deal of speculation, Franny."

Angela trembled at the sound of Lord Brynne's deep voice. She turned and saw him leaning against the door-frame in the nursery's entryway. He was dressed in pale grey pantaloons and glossy top-boots, and slate grey morning coat, a waistcoat of grey-and-wine-coloured paisley, and a neckcloth as white and crisp as new-fallen snow. His dark hair was a tumble of luxuriant waves, the sight of which made her fingers itch to sift through them. Fearful lest her fingers betray themselves, she hurriedly clasped them behind her back.

Lord Brynne stepped into the room, keenly watching her all the while. Despite her resolve to leave the Abbey, to remove herself from this enigma of a man, who pined for his late wife yet reputedly bedded all the most beautiful demi-reps in London, Angela was glad she'd taken extra care with her appearance that morning. Her abigail had helped her into one of her favourite and most becoming morning dresses. The white muslin, sprigged with roses and trimmed with silk ribbons of the same deep pink, made her feel especially feminine. She thought she saw appreciation simmering in the blue pools of his lordship's eyes, and her traitorous heart leapt with joy.

"I'm so sorry I didn't, my lord," said Fran, the maid's repentant voice breaking into Angela's trance-like state. She had forgotten all about Fran.

Lord Brynne pulled his eyes away from Angela and moved to stand next to Fran by the crib. "I know you are, Franny," he said not unkindly, smiling down at the maid. "But from now on you must be completely honest with me."

"Oh, I will, m'lord!" she assured him with a vigorous nod of her head.

"And how fares our smallest houseguest today?" he asked, reaching down to squeeze one of Harry's chubby knees. Harry gurgled delightedly, tossing his arms and legs in an energetic greeting.

"Sproutin' ivories like he's fixin' to eat your next leg o' lamb, my lord," Fran answered proudly.

Lord Brynne chuckled. "Good! However, by the time Harry's got his full set of ivories, he'll be sitting at another man's table."

Fran jerked her head to stare up at him. Angela was surprised, too, and waited expectantly for his next words. Evidently Lord Brynne had been busy that morning, making arrangements for Harry's future. But despite her questioning look, it would seem that Lord Brynne meant to deny her.

"Miss Fairfax, forgive me," he began, his eyes, too, conveying an apology, "but I must speak to Fran alone for a moment. Would you . . . ?"

Angela was quick to take the hint, though she could not help but wonder why the marquess felt the need to exclude her from any business concerning Harry. She did not think Fran would consider her presence intrusive. "Of course, my lord," she said quietly as she moved to the door.

"Why don't you go down to the blue parlour, Miss Fairfax?" he said before she could slip away completely. "I've made arrangements for us to have tea there in a few moments. There's a delightful view of the gardens and the lake beyond from the north window, and I thought it would be pleasant to move our little party in there for once."

Angela nodded mutely and walked downstairs, discovering from Lawrence the direction of the parlour Lord Brynne referred to. She went willingly enough because she felt in dire need of a good strong cup of tea. And if her papa was there already, she would press him again to move up their departure date. He would probably be there, because he generally did not take his first nap before he'd consumed his quota of tea and eaten a goodly number of the pastries and sandwiches which Mrs. Hobbs sent out with the tea-tray.

When Angela entered the room, it was empty. She had not expected to see Sir Timothy, because he was spending the day at the vicarage. She had heard how Lord Brynne had assured the vicar that Tim's oath of sobriety was not taken lightly, and how he had persuaded the suspicious vicar to give Tim a chance to prove himself. But where were her father and Lady Brynne?

Angela paced about the room, too nervous to sit down, and too nervous to stand still for more than a minute. It was a pretty room, decorated in pastel colours and light, elegant pieces of Chippendale furniture. Tea had been set out already, the china shining clean and bright and the usual delicacies placed attractively in several small dishes. And the view from the north window was indeed pleasant, the gentle slope of lawn smooth and green, and the sparkling surface of Derwentwater stretching like a shimmering royal robe to the distant shores.

Then it suddenly struck Angela that this room had a woman's touch. And with the sun neither setting nor rising directly into the room's largest window, it would be a pleasant chamber in which to sit to do stitchery or write letters. She wondered if it had been Caroline's sitting-room, and the possibility of this being the case produced a dull ache in her throat.

Indeed, if the Abbey *were* haunted, it was probably Caroline's spirit which walked the galleries! For how could any woman bear to leave such a lovely home, such a stirring and majestic country, and ... Yes, and most of all, how could any woman bear to leave a man like Lord Brynne?

"Miss Fairfax?"

For the second time that day Lord Brynne appeared on the scene unannounced, and Angela's taut nerves were nearly at the breaking-point. The scene outside the window blurred and she jerked round to face him, quite sure her nervousness showed plainly.

"I did not mean to alarm you, Miss Fairfax," said the marquess, his contrition obvious. "But I hardly slipped quietly into the room. In fact, I cleared my throat twice, but you seemed in a daze."

"I was thinking about ghosts, Lord Brynne," she explained, taking comfort in the half-truth. Then she tried to smile.

Lord Brynne raised one of his charmingly wicked-looking brows. "I thought you liked ghosts, my dear. Such a downcast look as I just observed on your face does not bespeak a mind fixed on pleasant thoughts. And your smile, so wan, so...forced!" He studied her for a moment, then said, "Perhaps I can tell you something which will lift your spirits."

"I am always willing to hear good news, my lord, though you are mistaken if you suppose I am the sort of missish girl who indulges in the megrims!" Angela staunchly informed him.

Lord Brynne looked sceptical and slightly amused, but he did not choose to argue the point, saying only, "Well then, here's some good news for you! Mr. Holmes asked my permission this morning to pay his addresses to Fran. Under normal circumstances, it would be quite unnecessary for him to apply to me, but he wishes to adopt Harry as his own and raise him as their first child. Fran has been more mother than sister to him, after all. I think it will serve very well and they will be exceedingly happy."

"Goodness, how can you inform me so calmly of these glad tidings!" exclaimed Angela, stepping quickly forward to clasp his hands. Then she just as quickly let go as she remembered how he'd responded the last time she'd seized his hands in a moment of impulsiveness. "Why, it settles everything so nicely! Fran and Harry shall be together, and Mr. Holmes... He does love her, doesn't he? He's not doing it out of some sense of pity or duty, is he?"

"No, he loves her, and has loved her for months, he says. I sometimes saw them together, but I never imagined that his affections had been so surely engaged. But he's a quiet fellow, not given to showing his feelings."

"Oh, I'm so glad! Now Harry will have a family of his own and settled near enough so that you can visit him!" This happy thought was followed immediately by the realization that she wouldn't be included in those pleasant visits.

Lord Brynne walked to the table and pulled out a chair, gesturing with one elegant hand for her to be seated. "There you are again—looking blue-devilled! Surely we can sort out these unpleasant thoughts and toss them to the wind. Tea, now that's the ticket! One can only wonder what great decisions have been made and what horrendous problems have been reduced to trifles over a good strong cup of tea, eh, Miss Fairfax?"

"Hadn't we ought to wait for the others, my lord?" she demurred, shrinking back a little.

He leaned forward and, like a mischievous boy imparting a secret, whispered gleefully, "The others aren't coming!"

"Wh-why not, my lord?" A tête-à-tête with his lordship did not seem at all wise to Angela.

"I shall tell you when you sit down," he said coaxingly.

"No, I don't think I should...."

"Or I can bodily lift you and sit you down like a recalcitrant child!" He made a small movement as if he were about to carry out his threat.

Angela moved quickly to the chair and sat down. She had no intention of discovering whether or not Lord Brynne was earnest in his threats. Besides, she did not want him to touch her, even with such an undignified purpose in mind. She might like it all too well and find herself swooning in his arms.

He sat down opposite her and smiled as a cat might grin at a cornered mouse.

"You aren't going to apologize to me again, are you?" she blurted out, tense with suspense.

Lord Brynne shook out his napkin and placed it neatly on his lap. "Oh, I would not dare to do that, Miss Fairfax. My apology was so ill received yesterday."

Not of a mind to be complaisant, she demanded, "Does my father know you arranged to meet me alone?"

"He certainly knows all, Miss Fairfax. More even than you, at this point. But if you will allow me to speak, perhaps it will become clear to you in the end."

"But—"

"Please, Miss Fairfax!"

Angela did not dare to speak again. Lord Brynne's eyes were alight with purpose and determination. Unnerved by his single-mindedness and afraid of what he might have to say, she reached out a trembling hand to clasp the handle of the teapot. She needed that cup of tea more than ever.

"Don't pour the tea, Miss Fairfax!" ordered the marquess, imprisoning her hand with his much larger one to keep her from lifting the teapot. Angela felt a pleasant tremor run up her arm. "At least, not yet," he amended in a gentler tone, removing his hand. "I can't think straight when I'm in my altitudes."

Angela carefully disentwined her fingers from the teapot handle and clutched them together in her lap. She did not know what to think of Lord Brynne's odd behaviour. Why, he spoke as though he thought the tea would make him bosky! And unless they made tea differently in the Lake Country, such an idea was quite singular. Angela sat very still and waited.

Lord Brynne looked pleased. "Is it possible, Miss Fairfax," he said with a crooked grin, "that I have reduced you to the shrinking violet who first sat at table with me? But fear not, I do not find such submissiveness attractive or necessary...."

Angela sat forward and opened her mouth to speak.

He raised his brows and lifted a restraining hand. "Except for today, if you please! I must have your complete, willing attention!"

Angela was struck by his sudden seriousness and she sat back, ready to listen and save her arguments and opinions for later.

"You said certain things to me yesterday which gave me great pause, Miss Fairfax," he began slowly and earnestly. "You made me re-examine my mode of life over the past two years. You made me want something...more. I was wrong to believe that true love can come only once to a man's life. And you have been the one to convince me of it."

Angela was sure she was dreaming. What was he saying? Did he truly believe now that he could cherish his past love for his first wife and still have room for another woman in his heart and life? And was that other woman...herself? Angela's throat felt parched, and she flicked out her tongue to wet her dry lips, trying hard to be as inconspicuous as possible. But even that small movement did not go unnoticed. The marquess looked at her lips and Angela felt them burn and tingle under his fiery scrutiny.

"When we kissed," he continued, his gaze never shifting, "I felt something reawaken inside me, something which had been dead for a long time." He lifted his eyes to hers. "You told me yesterday that you felt something, too. Did you, Angel?"

He'd called her "Angel"! And from his lips, she loved the whimsical endearment, even if she didn't deserve it! Now the ability Angela had developed over the past few days to tell farradiddles failed her utterly. Looking into those mesmerizing blue eyes, she could tell only the truth. "I did feel something. I felt something very strong indeed!" Then, wrenching her eyes away from his, she added, "But it does not signify how or what I felt, because even if you have come to terms with your past and now wish to pursue a present and a future, I still cannot marry you!"

The salt sting of tears against her eyelids made her blink. Turning her head aside, she willed herself to control the rising tide of emotions which had been threatening to overcome her all afternoon.

"And you have come to this conclusion because of my rogue's reputation. You have decided that I cannot be faithful to a wife," the marquess stated soberly.

"Indeed, I'd be a fool to think otherwise, wouldn't I? You are so handsome and are so used to having many different women—experienced women, too!" rasped Angela, choking on the painful lump which had formed in her throat. He wanted her and she daren't allow herself to marry him! What torture!

"I sought forgetfulness in pleasure, Angel," he told her earnestly. "I never loved, I never esteemed any of the women I've dallied with since Caroline died. And while she lived, I never felt the need, nor had the slightest desire, to make love to anyone but my wife! Why would I want an empty act of physical gratification over the sublime joining of body *and* soul? Angela, my dearest girl, I tell you this truly and ask you—with God as my witness!—to believe me!"

Angela raised her eyes to his, a large tear on one lash obscuring her vision so that she saw him as if through a prism. There were two of him, and both of them looked so sincere!

"Angel, my love," he continued, reaching forth to catch her hand and press it against his lips. "You told me when Harry was found that I should speak frankly and tell everyone that he wasn't my child. You said you were more likely to believe someone if they spoke 'plainly and promptly.' I cudgelled my brain all last night and this morning, wondering how I could convince you that I was faithful to my first wife and can and will be faithful to you if you would do me the great honour of marrying me! Then I remembered your words. I say it now, my love, *plainly and promptly,* there can never be, *will* never be anyone in my heart—or my bed—but you! I love you, Angel!"

Angela believed him. She believed him with all her heart and soul! And she hardly knew how to contain the resultant joy, except to leap to her feet and throw her arms about his dear neck! "I love you, too, Sydney!"

The ardour of her response was so strong as to topple over the marquess's chair and land them both on the floor in a most compromising tangle of arms and legs. Amidst Angela's squeal of surprise and his lordship's shout of deep-throated laughter, they unravelled themselves and pulled up to a sitting position on the Aubusson carpet covering the parlour floor. Then, as the merriment subsided and a sweeter emotion swelled in their breasts, Lord Brynne pulled his naughty angel into his arms and kissed her softly, lingeringly, urgently, capably.

Breathless moments later, with the marquess's one hand curved round Angela's neck and the other just about to cup her bottom, Angela murmured reluctantly against the lips of her betrothed, "Perhaps we'd better take tea, Sydney, my love, before we are discovered carousing on the floor!"

Quite sure she would be disappointing her beloved by curtailing their lovemaking, Angela was surprised by the strange light in Sydney's eyes at the mention of tea and the prompt way he stood up and helped her to her feet.

"A capital idea!" he said, straightening his waistcoat, which had been twisted till the buttons were sadly askew and tugging at his mussed cravat as if it weren't quite beyond fixing. Angela straightened her own attire and watched, fascinated, as her dishevelled fiancé sat down to the tea-table with the sort of eagerness that one usually reserved for monumental events such as a visit from royalty, for example, or the total eclipse of the sun, perhaps.

But when she prepared to sit down opposite him, he caught her hand and pulled her onto his knee. "But Sydney," she objected, though she was secretly pleased to know he was not so easily distracted from their lovemaking, "I thought we were going to drink tea!"

"We are, my love," he assured her, giving her a squeeze. "And I have been picturing us taking tea together, just so, for days now. I adore the way you take tea! Pour, my Angel, in your usual captivating style. But no sugar, please. If I find the brew a trifle bitter for my tastes, I shall sweeten it up nicely in the manner I find most pleasing!" Then he kissed her again and nibbled on her ear as if it were the tastiest brandy-snap imaginable.

"Cream?" she asked him between gasps of sinful ecstasy.

"No, I do not like cream in my tea," he returned, chuckling. "Nor do I like it on the front of my shirt!"

Angela turned bemusedly to observe her beloved's soiled shirt-front, doused, as it were, with several splashes of cream. "I begin to perceive, Sydney, that tea may be a messy affair in our house!"

Sydney laughed, the joyous sound vibrating through the room and settling, finally, in the sweet, sacred chambers of his large heart. "Set down the cream, Angel, and pass the sugar," he ordered.

Angela puckered her lips, more than willing to oblige.

EPILOGUE

August 1818

MADELINE FAIRFAX, Lady Amesbury, sat at her dressing-table and carefully applied a dab of rouge to the middle of each cheek, rubbing it in with practised strokes. Then she lifted a flagon of costly Parisian scent and doused herself generously with it. Her dressing-gown was a gossamer wisp of pale blue which exactly matched her eyes. She stood and turned from side to side, considering the fall of the material about her slender hips and adjusting the *décolletage* to expose just a smidge more of white bosom.

Satisfied at last, she moved to the bed, which was hung with blue damask bedcurtains which had been made according to her own precise specifications, and settled herself amongst the satin bedclothes.

She had not long to wait. Presently there was a soft knock at the door which connected her bedchamber with her husband's. She quickly picked up a book from the bedside table and pretended to be reading as Lord Amesbury entered the room.

"Maddy, are you reading, my raisin tart?"

"Oh, it's you, Percy! I did not flatter myself that you would pay me a visit tonight since we leave so early in the morning for Castlerigg! You find me completely unprepared to receive you, my love!" She smiled seductively.

Lord Amesbury returned her come-hither smile with a wolfish grin and galumphed eagerly to the bed. Wriggling under the bedclothes, he pulled his wife into his arms and affixed his lips to hers.

Pulling herself free for a moment and propping her hands against her husband's huge chest, Lady Amesbury said, "Percy, my charger, do you think Angela will like my gift for the baby?"

"Why wouldn't she, my pomegranate?" he replied, breathing hard.

"Well, it has been a long time since I've been obliged to buy a christening gift for a grandchild. And just so Wellesley is not envious of his little sister, I've bought him a gift, too. But then, Wellesley's such a good boy. And he likes his new mama so well, and accepted her so readily when she and Sydney married last year, I don't really think he'll be envious of the baby. Do you?"

Stretching his short, fat neck to kiss the scented hollow behind her ladyship's small, shell-shaped ear, Lord Amesbury grunted, "I'm not at all worried about Wellesley! Angela loves him as if he were hers, and he knows it, too. What I dread is another of Beakman's sermons. I grow tired of hearing about the Evils of Deception and Judging Not That Ye Be Not Judged! He has never forgotten Joseph's betrayal, or forgiven Angela for thinking him Harry's father! Demmed hypocrite, ain't he?''

Gasping daintily as her husband trailed a finger along the lace edging of her bodice, Lady Amesbury nodded agreement. "True, my love. But except for that tiresome vicar, I quite look forward to visiting the Abbey. It was such a good notion of mine to take Angela there last autumn, wasn't it, Percy? But if I hadn't convinced Sydney to marry her by demonstrating how wonderful it is to fall in love again, it might never have come to anything, after all! Don't you agree, my tiger?''

"Yes, Maddy, you did it all!" Lord Amesbury returned readily. "And if Angela had not gone to the Abbey, Sir Timothy might not be happily wed to Charity, either. I hear she's with child, too!''

"Don't forget Fran Holmes, Percy. Their babe comes two months after Charity and Tim's! Harry needs a little brother or sister; he's becoming dreadfully spoiled! But though they all wed within a month of one another, don't you think it rather fitting that Sydney sired the first offspring among them? He was always such a good boy, and has always been so very capable in anything he undertook to accomplish!''

"I daresay it runs in the family, Maddy," observed Lord Amesbury, fast becoming frustrated. "Now would you please shut up and let me make love to you?''

Lady Amesbury shuddered with exquisite pleasure. "Percy, you're such a beast!''

HARLEQUIN
PROUDLY PRESENTS
A DAZZLING NEW CONCEPT IN ROMANCE FICTION

One small town—twelve terrific love stories

Welcome to Tyler, Wisconsin—a town full of people
you'll enjoy getting to know, memorable friends and
unforgettable lovers, and a long-buried secret that
lurks beneath its serene surface....

JOIN US FOR A YEAR IN THE LIFE OF TYLER

Each book set in Tyler is a self-contained love story;
together, the twelve novels stitch the fabric of a
community.

LOSE YOUR HEART TO TYLER!

The excitement begins in March 1992, with
WHIRLWIND, by Nancy Martin. When lively, brash
Liza Baron arrives home unexpectedly, she moves
into the old family lodge, where the silent and
mysterious Cliff Forrester has been living in seclusion
for years....

WATCH FOR ALL TWELVE BOOKS
OF THE TYLER SERIES
Available wherever Harlequin books are sold

TYLER-G